LOVESONGS OF EMMANUEL TAGGART

LOVESONGS OF

To Kris & Tanya

EMMANUEL TAGGART

a novel

SYR RUUS

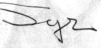

love,

Syr

LIBRARY AND ARCHIVES CANADA CATALOGUING IN PUBLICATION

Ruus, Syr
   Lovesongs of Emmanuel Taggart / Syr Ruus.
ISBN 978-1-55081-263-3
   I. Title.
PS8635.U96L69 2009   C813'.6   C2009-900835-1

Cover Design: Erin Cossar
Layout: Rhonda Molloy

BREAKWATER BOOKS LTD. acknowledges the support of the Canada Council
for the Arts which last year invested $20.1 million in writing and publishing
throughout Canada. We acknowledge the financial support of the Government of
Canada through the Book Publishing Industry Development Program for our
publishing activities. We acknowledge the financial support of the Government of
Newfoundland and Labrador through the department of Tourism, Culture and
Recreation for our publishing activities.

Printed in Canada

TO MY LOVING FAMILY

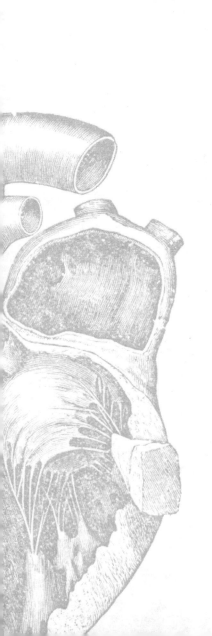

1

ONE morning in early February at precisely 10:42 a.m., Emmanuel Taggart turned a corner. Idling at his cluttered desk, he became mesmerized by the thin red line of the second hand jerking its way around the pale face of the office clock, feeling all of his life energy drain out of him. From brain to torso. Fizzling through his convoluted intestines. Down numb legs to splayed feet. Seeping from the soles of his leather boots, through the green plastic tiles of the floor to the pink insulation below, disappearing without as much as a gurgle into the fibrous mass. Head heavy with emptiness, eyes teary and sore, mouth slack-jawed and open, perhaps drooling, pounding temples cradled in limp hands, he desired nothing more than to lie down on the floor. In the locked stall of a public washroom, preferably, with its thick smell of disinfectant covering up more primal odours, the soothing hum of the fan above. No one demanding anything of him; everyone involved in his own private business, or patiently waiting with dripping hands at the hot air dispenser.

"Lordy, Mr. Taggart. You don't look so good."

It was Rose, his secretary.

No response. A faint flutter of eyelids.

"Something's going around," she chirruped. "Everyone's getting it."

He managed a mumble. "Gotta go home." Yet nothing in his entire life of forty-five years had ever seemed as difficult as to rise up from his chair, push his leaden arms into the sleeves of his winter jacket and wobble on rubbery legs down the hallway. Luckily there was an elevator. The cold air outside revived him enough to manage the distance through the parking lot to his car.

"Christ!" he exclaimed, but the invocation brought no release from his anguish.

Immobile behind the wheel, huddled into the chrome-blue, down-filled greatcoat, his own warmth slowly creeping over him, he began to notice the world once again. Bare trees outlined against a white sky. A single crow making its way from one side of the windshield's frame to the other. He pulled up the hood of the jacket and snuggled in, an ancient turtle viewing a shadowy landscape barely visible now through the fogged up windows, the black cement of parking lot marked off in faded yellow rectangles rimmed by a ridge of dirty snow. Soon even these indications disappeared. In grey solitude he sat, his shoulders hunched into his heart, expelling his life force in bursts of hot air which tickled the edges of his moustache.

His wife Emily hated it, the coat. Didn't appreciate the colour, the cut. Didn't like the image he had wrought for himself of late. Not up to her standards of style. Too cheap. He had bought it after Christmas at Wal-Mart on sale. If she still thought that clothes made a man, so be it. After years of pretence, he didn't care. HE DIDN'T

CARE! He would go naked into the world.

A tap on the window interrupted these permutations.

Reluctantly he pushed his head out of the bright warm shell, a balding and vulnerable protrusion, large red ears exposed. Three more sharp raps by the left one. Sotto voice raised in alarm. He rubbed off some of the condensation with his fingers to reveal a bright O of red lips embracing yellowish crooked teeth. The mouth of his secretary, Rose. Parents should have invested in braces when she was a child. Neglectful, he thought, or more than likely, poor.

The lips moving now, a sea-urchin under water seeking nourishment. "Are you all right?" he heard faintly through the glass.

Rubbing some more at the window to include two black eyebrows upraised over dark brown eyes full of concern. Why was Rose following him outside like this in the middle of winter?

She moved her hand in a rapid circular motion indicating he should roll down the window.

A-OK. Circling thumb and index finger, winking his right eye, making sure she noticed the gesture by twisting up his mouth under the moustache. That should do it, he assured himself, but she knocked again vigorously and motioned once more about the window.

What lay ahead of him now seemed like a task of such magnitude that sweat broke out upon his brow and he took a couple of deep breaths to brace himself. No longer, in this modern age, could one simply turn a crank to open a car window as Rose had intimated. That was outmoded, out of style, only maintained for the unfortunate minority still poor enough to live a simple life which afforded no options. For the majority, the procedure had become much more demanding: First one had to dig out the car keys from a trouser pocket and then find the ignition to turn on the motor before the damned power switch would work. If it indeed it did work. If it wasn't frozen up. Or broken.

"Are you all right?" she repeated.

Panting with exhaustion from his efforts, the cold air from the open window slapping vigorously across his hot face, he stared at this woman he had seen many times every day, who now seemed like an apparition from a former existence he had no interest in reclaiming.

"I looked out and saw your car still sitting here in the lot. Then I started thinking you weren't feeling so good and maybe you passed out or something, and I says to myself, Rose, you better check this out. And here you still are, Mr. Taggart. Are you okay? You don't look so good." Shivering. Pulling her coat together to protect her scrawny neck, sleeves blowing empty at the sides.

He managed a few nods, jerking his head about as he started the car.

"Should I call your wife?" Rose inquired, backing away.

He made the sign again, A-OK, and left her standing there in the parking lot holding on to her coat with bare-knuckled purplish hands, stamping high heels against the pavement in little hops. Glancing in the rear-view mirror before he pulled out into the traffic, he saw her scurry back to the building, a little mouse seeking sanctuary. His secretary, Rose, clicking the computer keys with long painted fingernails, bright-winged insects exploring an arid land. She always removed her glasses and swiped the back of her skirt with her hand a few times to straighten things out before coming to his desk. Breath stinking of coffee and cigarettes.

Should give up smoking, Rose. More women are dying of lung cancer these days than have breasts removed. A fact he had picked up on the documentary channel.

I know, I know, she says, pushing scraggly black bangs off her forehead. *It's so hard to quit once you start.*

He pressed cruise control, Rose's flower face following him down the highway, three deep wrinkles between the brows from squinting without her glasses, scapulas protruding through her sweater, the back of her white neck dotted with black stubble after her appointment with the hairdresser. Asked to leave early on those days. Three-thirty.

She was efficient enough, though her manner had always irritated him. Servile. Harried. Agitated. Lipstick on her teeth. Not one of those young, curvy, luscious secretaries they wrote into sitcoms. Which perhaps was a good thing, since he had always prided himself as a family man, not the kind to be tempted. A dependable provider, a supportive father to his sons, chin up, shoulders squared, ready to share a joke or lend a helping hand when needed. A good Joe, a square dealer, a responsible citizen, a fair though somewhat distant boss, as respectability demanded. But now, Rose's image as she had appeared in his rear-view mirror took hold of him. Running out into the icy cold in those tiny high-heeled shoes to make sure he was all right. He'd never thought much about her private life before.

A grainy documentary appeared on the small screen of his colourless brain: *Rose raising a slack arm to hit the snooze button for another five minutes of blissful sleep. First up in the apartment, smelly with cigarette butts and stale exhalations. Scuzzy tongue over algaed teeth. Swampy morning breath. Hacking up phlegm. Her face*

erased of the dark eyebrows and red lips. It's ten after,
she shouts. The kids have their own alarms, but they
depend on their mother. Every day begins with an
argument. Clearing the table in front of the TV. It's
something anyway, she remarks to her unseen audience,
to make the place look halfway decent, like wearing clean
underwear just in case you end up in Emergency. With
agile fingers she collects the refuse: three glasses in one
hand; a large plastic bowl containing unpopped kernels and
crumpled napkins in the other.

Seven-fifteen, she hollers. Let's go! Let's go! Let's go!
She has a few minutes to herself yet as she places the dirty
dishes into the sink and runs water over them. At least
lunch-making is done with, the kids both in high school.
All they want now is money. She counts out two piles of
three loonies each, remembering to get change every night
before coming home from work. If she left more, enough
for a week, say, on Monday mornings, they would spend it
on something else. Maybe they do even now, but it isn't
her fault. She's doing the best she can, on her own with
those two. Though Amelia's skinny as a beanpole and
Royce might already be smoking. Cigarettes or dope?
Probably both. It's hard to tell with the gum he chews.

Thus preoccupied with the imagined daily life of his
secretary, warmly ensconced in his downy blue cocoon,
the motor softly throbbing, the car on cruise, Emmanuel
missed Exit 13 to his own home in Banbury altogether.

2

"I'LL be damned," he mumbled, suddenly aware again of his own existence as he watched the sign for Exit 17 speed by. For a moment he considered a U-turn across the snow-covered median of the four-lane highway, but didn't dare take the chance. There was some sort of new radar now, he'd heard. A computer tracking one's every move. He would just drive to the next exit, then double back. It was still early. The clock on the dashboard showed 3:45. Plenty of time yet before Emily got home. In case Rose *had* called, the answering machine blinking unheeded in the empty house. *Your husband, he don't look so good.*

Hot now in his puffy coat, swiping a wet forehead, alert for road signs. Passing through a poor landscape of shallow, rocky soil. Drab fields of dead grass. Clumps of scaggy evergreens. *Barren and neglected. Barren and neglected.* The words repeating themselves over and over before eventually fading out, leaving his thoughts folded up neatly, stacked together like a pile of unused sheets in a linen closet. Almost missing it again, the next exit, pressing his foot down hard on the brake, squealing the tires, having to back up nevertheless on the shoulder of the road, luckily there was no oncoming traffic, rounding the wide curve to the stop sign and taking a left.

It should have been simple to turn himself around: a left and then a right or perhaps another left and you're back on the highway, heading in the opposite direction. That's what you were supposed to do. But then again, maybe this far out of the city things were different. No cloverleaves here. You got off the highway in one town and couldn't get on again until the next. Still, there were always signs. Unless he had totally missed them, which wasn't altogether impossible, given his present condition. Uncomfortable and itchy, sweat pouring down beneath his downy insulation, *fucking Jesus Christ*, nearing five already, pressing hard on the accelerator with no idea in the world where he was going.

Strangely enough, it all looked vaguely familiar. The small rise ahead through that clump of trees, the road curving slightly to the left revealing a patch of grey sky, sullen and moist; he would have to watch out for black ice later, a flash back to his youth, hurrying to get home before the curfew, driving too fast, his life not as important as the consequences of being late.

Dusk settling in. At this rate he'd never make it back before Emily came home to the dark empty house, whatever had been there vanishing quickly, diminishing into the shadows at the click of the key. Always a strangeness lingering in the air, the red button by the telephone flashing its urgent message, until the lights were turned on, the thermostat turned up, the bags of groceries piled haphazardly on the kitchen table, boots off and standing guard on the mat by the front door, blustery commonplace human energy taking charge once again, driving everything else into hiding. Yet no place was ever empty just because man wasn't there to overpower it with his cumbersome presence. Why hadn't he ever considered that possibility before?

Five-fifteen. Still nothing. Not a sign, not a house, not even a place to turn around. Just this lonely country road with its soft shoulders, forging its godforsaken way through the scraggly forest. Deep ditches on either side. If he went over the bank here, it would take months before anyone discovered the wreck. Maybe years. Perhaps they would never find him. Peacefully unconscious, hanging upside down in the crumpled vehicle hidden by dense undergrowth. A missing man. Last seen by his secretary, Rose, leaving the office at approximately 11 a.m. The subject of frantic phone calls, his boys flying home. Even now his lips curved upward at the thought of his sons, until he remembered the imagined circumstances of their unexpected visit, and a sudden taste of salty tears stung his sinuses. Have a happy life, my dear boys, he wished with all his heart. *A long life and an easy death*, his mother used to sigh, suckling her lower lip and nodding her head sagely, *that's the best anyone can hope for.*

But it could very well be otherwise. He might be trapped. Stuck in that damnable ditch for days, able to move three fingers of his right hand. Desperately waiting for someone, anyone, to save him. The authorities wouldn't begin the search for several days. In case he had just decided to run away.

That last terrifying image of his terminal breath brought him out of his torpor. For a good twenty minutes now he had been driving down this deserted road, heading nowhere. It was nearly dark. At the next likely spot, he would turn around and go back the way he came. But then he did see something ahead. A beacon from the depths. Embossed within a cube of severed forest, a porch light beaming warmly upon the front steps of a small white bungalow. Relieved, he pulled into the driveway. But as he put the car into reverse and opened the door a crack so he could see to back up, a woman appeared on the porch, waving one of her arms in large frantic circles.

Quickly he yanked the gearshift back into Park and opened the door wider but couldn't quite make out what she wanted. Was she in trouble? A domestic altercation? An emergency? She seemed so agitated that, in spite of his own unstable condition, his better nature compelled him to shut off the motor and heave his bulk out into the cold to find out what he could do to help. But as he got closer, he noted with surprise that she was smiling.

"We've been waiting for you," she shouted. "Come on in!"

From behind the knees of her faded jeans, two faces peeked out, blue-eyed and pink with excitement.

"This is Sara." She indicated the taller one. "And this little one here is Penny. They're a bit shy," she apologized. "And that big feller sitting over there," she said, pointing her chin at a large tan dog scrutinizing him with his ears cocked, "that's Deal. Good Deal," she called as the dog approached, tail wagging broadly, snuffling at Emmanuel's legs.

"Here, let me take your coat," she offered.

What could he say? There was nothing he could think of, except to hand over the encumbrance and follow them into the living room like a wordless robot, the little girls giggling and dancing around him.

"How about a cold brew," she offered, "before dinner? You look like you could use one." Without waiting for an answer, she disappeared into the kitchen.

Sara and Penny huddled together on the sofa opposite him, the dog at their feet, all three solemnly staring. He smelled cooking in the air. Garlic and tomato sauce. Definitely something Italian.

The woman returned with a large glass pitcher full of foamy dark beer and two tall glasses. "I've been making it regular since John's gone. Not too good for the figure." She patted the back of her jeans. "But it gets one through the nights." Carefully she filled the glasses, leaving a scum of sediment in the bottom of the pitcher. It tasted sweet and a bit yeasty but quite refreshing after one got used to it.

"And as for you loverly ladies..." She turned to the girls. "Some purple Kool-Aid fit for a queen. How's that? But you've got to be careful not to spill any, okay?"

She left again and the little girls wiggled with anticipation as if something altogether wonderful was about to happen, holding each other by the hand, but still keeping four big blue eyes focused on their guest.

He was beginning to feel like a Santa who had mislaid his sack.

"Here you are, my loverlies," the woman said, returning with two glasses half filled with bright purple.

She seemed about thirty, give or take, he figured, haggard-looking, heavy-lidded Mongolian eyes in a Nordic face, dark blond hair hanging raggedly down her neck, a smear of lipstick. Could have been a looker in her prime, he supposed, although for years he hadn't cultivated much of an eye for women.

For awhile they all sipped in silence. When the girls were done, the bigger one took the glasses and positioned them carefully on the coffee table. Then they both resumed their silent staring, their lips and tongues purple.

"Hope you like lasagne," the mother said. "Every once in awhile I get an urge to cook up something special."

He nodded and stretched his lips into a smile, surreptitiously turning up his left wrist to glance at his watch. Six o'clock, almost. Time for him to be home. Emily would have dinner ready by now, baked potatoes and boneless skinless chicken breasts in the microwave, not bothering to cook much anymore for just the two of them with the boys gone, wondering why he was late. Unless Rose had called and left a message. The red eye blinking, the bad news received. Then she would be worried. Where was he? According to his secretary he had left the office hours ago not looking so good. They should have investigated cell phones, but neither of them had ever been adventurous with technology.

Really he must be going, he meant to say, but looking at the three faces, cheery and expectant, he couldn't make the words come out of his mouth.

"You must be pretty hungry. Why don't you take your glass right to the table," she told him. "I'll open a coupla more bottles. Beer goes good with Italian."

The table, covered with a red-checked tablecloth, was already set in a small alcove off the kitchen.

"You sit there," she instructed Emmanuel while pulling up a highchair for one child and settling the other into a green plastic booster seat. Then she lit the candles and turned off the overhead light.

"Can I blow them out, Mama? Please? When we're done," Sara asked shyly, her eyes still on the guest.

Penny, grown used to his presence, was banging cheerfully on her tray with a spoon.

The dinner looked spectacular: an enormous platter of lasagne creamy with cheese, a big bowl of Caesar salad topped by large curls of crispy bacon, thick slices of toasted garlic bread.

"Eat. Eat," she ordered. "Drink up." Preoccupied cutting the pasta into little pieces for the girls, jumping up because she forgot the milk, pouring beer from the pitcher, feeding the baby, hardly taking time to eat a bite herself, no chance to take much notice of him.

"Bad Deal," she said, shaking a finger at the dog. "Don't beg. Out. Out. Go lie down."

To be polite, Emmanuel chewed and swallowed, but his stomach was not in the mood to accept anything and his mind was busy trying to formulate an acceptable getaway. When dinner was over, then what? Undoubtedly there would come a time he would have to reveal himself as an impostor, not the man she was expecting. Would there be a scene in front of these little girls, their faces now smeared with spaghetti sauce and sporting hearty milk moustaches?

She apologized for the dessert, couldn't think of anything proper to go with Italian, as she brought in a homemade lemon pie towering high with meringue. There was no way he could decline that, though the table was still laden with food when they finished and Sara was finally permitted to stand up on a chair to blow out the candles.

"We'll leave all this for later," she said. "You just settle yourself down in the living room with a cup of coffee and I'll get these little rapscallions to bed. Then we can talk."

Forever after he was ashamed of what he did next. When the water upstairs began to run, hearing the squeals and splashes of the little girls in their bath, with the brown eyes of the big dog following his every movement, he put down his cup, tiptoed to the hallway and picked up his coat. Remembering the pet of his childhood, old Rufus, who greeted people with frantic tail wagging and barked only when anyone left, he put his finger to his lips. *No Deal.* Then he went out the door, closing it softly behind him. Under the circumstances he could think of nothing else he could do. Without turning on the car lights, he backed out the driveway, a pain in his gut and despair like a leaden weight consuming what was left of his brain.

Yet he had no trouble finding the entrance ramp back to the highway. It was, indeed, directly beside where he had come off, its very closeness making the turn unremarkable. Like a stone, he sat behind the wheel, the car on Cruise, driving itself. Numbly he pulled into his own driveway, watching the garage door automatically open as his headlights activated the switch. He couldn't allow himself to think about any of it, going in to meet his wife's anxious face, angry at first, then softening when she finally got a good look at him.

"Where have you been?" she demanded, taking the coat from his arms. "You look absolutely terrible."

"I got lost," he managed, before starting to blubber like a baby.

3

SHE made him take two extra-strength Tylenol with a cup of hot milk, and he remembered nothing else until he felt her arm reach over him to shut off the alarm. Usually he was the first one up, bright and purposeful at six, making a small fire in the airtight, measuring out coffee – decaf: better for the heart – whistling softly to himself, listening to the news while he ate his customary bowl of bran flakes – to keep his bowels regular and prevent colon cancer. Looking forward to yet another day in the life of Emmanuel "M" Taggart, a jolly, good-natured fellow, a regular guy, always ready to help, to cheer on, to share a laugh, to give a hand, someone to depend upon, a good citizen, a proud father, a supportive husband.

But where was he now? What had happened to him?

Pretending sleep, he sensed her careful movements as she got ready for work. Inching the pantyhose up her legs, tucking in the flap of tummy, hooking the bra in front before turning it around to fit herself in, pulling the straps over her shoulders, a small mound of flesh appearing on both sides of the armpits. Thickening into middle age, Emily, his wife.

Em and Em. Big M and little m. M & m.

Fully dressed now in makeup and coat, she tiptoed back upstairs. "M?" she whispered, brushing his cheek imperceptibly with the tips of her fingers, a loving touch he would never have felt had he really been asleep, as she set down a glass of orange juice and the container of Tylenol pills on the nightstand beside the bed.

He opened his lids slightly, barely lifting his chin from the pillow.

"I'm leaving for work now. You sleep. I'll call Rose later and check in with you at lunchtime. Okay?" Smacking her lips in a kiss.

A finality in the clack of the front door. Shortly after, her car pulling out of the driveway. He was alone at last. Still, he waited a few moments to make sure she was really gone before raising himself on one elbow to listen. Was it indeed true, as he had always suspected, that unseen presences took possession of a house when everyone was gone? Was something even now interloping the empty living room, the vacant kitchen, dirty breakfast dishes soaking in the sink, not aware of him still and silent in the night-smelling bed? But though he listened with both his ears, he heard nothing.

Wide awake now, he turned his pillow secretively to the fresh side and watched his toes appear from beneath the bottom of the covers, strangers he hardly ever saw. Pale and fleshless. The second one, long and skinny, hunched over from years of hunkering down in socks and shoes. His ankles white, weak-looking, his calves covered sparsely in black hair, like an Arctic forest, his gastrocnemius slack. But soon the hum of his own silence soothed him asleep once again, a deep dreamless deadening sleep, so heavy that when the phone rang, he was certain he was being restrained within a brilliantly illuminated torture chamber enduring the technique of sleep deprivation so he would tell them everything he knew. Two weeks without sleep would kill a healthy rat, he read somewhere.

"Mmmfh," he wuffled into the receiver just before the answering machine took over.

"My God, M, you sound terrible. Should I take the rest of the day off and come home?"

"Sleeping," he said. "Still sleeping."

"It's the flu," she reassured him. "Drink some juice, take some more Tylenol, stay in bed. Do you ache all over? Do you have a fever? Is your nose runny? Is your throat sore?" she questioned with doctoral authority.

"None of the above," he answered. "Just tired is all. Don't worry. I'll rest today and be up and wagging tomorrow."

He had answered truthfully. What he hadn't told her was that his whole head was vibrating and his real life seemed small and faraway: binocular vision from the big end. But he did as he was told – two extra-strength Tylenol downed with a glass of orange juice – settling in once more under the covers, flat on his back, immersed in the bright but insubstantial afternoon light of February foreshadowing a frozen night.

Real sleep was no longer possible. Lingering in the dim zone between sleep and wakefulness, the realm of dreamlike vision where images faded one to another with no consequences, he dared approach her again. Uneven strands of dark blond hair on the back of her neck. Pouring out beer not good for the figure, patting herself lightly on her tight jeans, *John is gone*, she said. Where was he then? Not gone forever, surely, deserting those cherubic little girls and that accommodating woman.

And where had he himself been anyway? It all seemed so unreal. Given this sudden breakdown in his usually well-functioning system, could it be that he had imagined the whole encounter while speeding robotically down the highway to destinations unknown? But why? *WHAT IS HAPPENING TO ME!*

He sat up, rubbed his head and face vigorously, and scrutinized the familiar bedroom, the blue-flowered wallpaper with its matching trim, lacy curtains reforming a white winter sky, two dark walnut bureaus filled with underwear and socks, part of the bedroom suite they bought on time when they first married. Emily keen on nesting when the boys were small, painting and papering, trimming and stencilling around windows and doors. Stitching up pillowcases and curtains. A course in re-upholstering. Scavenging antique stores and yard sales. Refinishing the junk she dragged home. *What do you think?* she would ask him. *Nice*, he said a long time ago, *very nice*, not really looking then, but seeing now. She had done a good job. Patterns matched up evenly, the seams hardly noticeable. *Good work, Em.* Should have appreciated it more at the time but he was too busy making his own mark, for the boys, for their future, certain his opinions counted, his efforts were important, his worry made a difference. Mike and Gerry, his sons, gone now, gone like John, building their own futures, the actual living Dad in his down-filled chrome-blue greatcoat an embarrassment, an intrusion, an interference, an obligation in their newly independent lives.

So fast, it went by so fast. *I hardly had the time to measure your distance, to hold you in my arms, to be able to touch you, to kiss you, to throw you high into the air and hear you laugh, to hold you both by the hand and see you look up at me. Dad's home! What do you do, Dad, when you go away? Me, son? I'm a paper pusher, son. Right on, Dad!* Then it was over, his boys nearly grown with eyes beginning to doubt, to formulate judgments: *You're out of date, Dad, out of style, out of line, you could have done better, Dad, maybe you could have done more, but we know you tried, Dad, it's just that things are different nowadays, people don't push paper anymore, people are more hip, Dad, more with it, we know what's going on, life changes, Dad, time marches on, you just don't understand, Dad. YOU DON'T LISTEN.*

Big M and little m, dregs left behind, Dad prone now under a flower-strewn down-filled duvet, his white upturned belly sparsely covered with black hair turning grey, thickening down below. He lifted the covers and raised up the band of his pyjama bottoms, but it was just as he expected, his unit resting serenely on its cushion of fur, better not disturb it. Poking his finger here and there into his flesh, he discovered that it did hurt; he was, indeed, surprisingly tender.

He threw aside the bedclothes and went to the bathroom to conduct a more thorough examination. Unless the scale was wrong, weight well over two hundred pounds, far above the limit he had set for himself several years ago. In the mirror, his face flaccid, definitely sickly. Dull strands of reddish hair combed over an enlarging forehead, his virility eroding, leaving behind brown spots he had dismissed as freckles. Eyes drowning in wrinkles, the whites rheumy, pale pink under the lower lid, anemic. Breath sour, probably from all that garlic and beer he had consumed the evening before, if indeed he had actually been there and done that. Tongue coated in white mould, left too long in the cupboard. Throat a bit infected, he thought, but it was possible it always looked like that. Head filled with lead, poisoned, so heavy he could hardly support it cupped in his hands, his elbows on his knees, sitting down on the toilet to pee like a girl.

4

MAYBE he *was* getting the flu, as Em had predicted. Comforted by the thought, he went back to bed, pillow over his face to shut out the light. But the beating of his heart kept him awake. It seemed erratic, laboured. After forty-five years of this constant thumping and pumping, how long could it last? His father's first heart attack occurred in his mid-forties. The children called suddenly home from college. Dad comatose in hospital, hooked up to tubes; Mom distraught and weeping. Six weeks he spent in bed. Another year recovering. Couldn't go back to his former job as a shipping clerk. Too stressful, the deadlines, the customer complaints. From the large end of the binoculars his dad appeared diminished, red hair dulled to grey, short legs supporting his long torso, years of Mom's meatloaf, Fritos crunched in front of the TV, ice cream with chocolate sauce before bed, emerging transformed to push out his golfing shirt above his Bermuda shorts like a symbol of middle-class morality. *They broke the mould after they made Dad*, his mother would say. Always Emmanuel had felt this as a reprimand. He never could measure up to the old man.

Not that he wanted to. His rebellion conducted privately in secret, the smile on his face as phony as his father's when the old man jollied waitresses or joked with the garbage men, making his adolescent son wince with embarrassment, a do-gooder, a church-goer, waking him up once in the middle of the night when he was little, his mother standing as silent witness, Dad sitting on the bed solemnly saying, *I'll never drink again, I promise, son.*

What had happened to bring him to that? Emmanuel wondered. What horrible sin had he committed? He would never know. It was too late to ask. Dad becoming religious then. Piously opinionated. Saving and scrimping all their lives, both of them working so the children could get their educations and have a better life. After the heart attack, staying home with his special diet, his bottles of pills, lounging in his imitation leather recliner where he fell asleep in front of the TV watching bowling or golf. Every once in awhile the old temper would flare up, erupting for no reason, because the tea was cold, the sugar not on the table, because his daughter was pregnant and had to get married, showing his true colours then, his face bright purple, digging up the garden like a madman though he wasn't supposed to exert himself. Some fire in the old guy yet, even if most of the time he acted like a prissy nun and walked with a cane, and the only job he was still fit for was night watchman at the factory, part-time.

How could he, their only son, have been so unfeeling, so insensitive, so ignorant of their lives, their hopes, their dreams for their children, judging them as harshly as he did? Only now he understood. He wished he could tell him: *Dad, they broke the mould when they made you.* Too late, always too late. Dad's heart finally giving away despite the skimmed milk and margarine. Pain of unshed tears beneath the lids.

Emmanuel bit his lip hard under the moustache. Got up and took two more extra-strength Tylenol. Fell asleep then once again, dreaming he was a little boy looking up at his father's large ruddy face, holding his hand, walking home from a baseball game across a green lawn under a clear blue summer sky. Stopping in at the pub for a cool one, sitting on the counter drinking pop. *Hey, Pat, that your boy? You got yourself a fine-looking lad there.*

Then someone erasing the dream, forcing him awake, calling out his name. The smell of winter, of the outdoors, of life going on as usual without him. Emily, his wife, home from work, her coat still on, the windows of the bedroom black with darkness, the overhead light unbearably bright through his lashes.

"I had a terrible nightmare," he said, sweaty and disoriented. "I was being tortured. They wouldn't let me sleep until I told them what I knew and I didn't know anything."

"You told me that already," she said, placing a cool hand on his brow. "Must be a recurring dream. It's common with fever."

But when she took his temperature it was normal. Slightly below, in fact. "Maybe you sweated it out," she said.

She heated up a can of chicken noodle soup for him, but the slimy white noodles and tasteless bits of dead chicken made him feel nauseated. In the den, sprawled out on the couch, he watched TV mindlessly, with little consciousness of what occurred on the screen, irritated to hot fury by the canned laughter, the insipid music, the same ads appearing over and over again, someone not doing his job, asleep at the controls. If he had more energy he would have heaved something through the screen, caused an explosion, screams, the sound of breaking glass. *What was that, my love? Oh, nothing, my dear. It is but the beginning of the destruction I am prepared to hurl upon the world and everyone in it. Behold the wrath of Emmanuel, all ye who dare to step into his awesome presence.*

When she went to bed, he turned off the sound altogether and watched the pictures until they too faded out. His brain was no longer located at the top of his head but had shifted downward, consumed and digested by his body, his skull empty, only the hollows of the eye sockets remaining as evidence that he had once been a human being who had seen and remarked upon what went on in his world.

5

TOMORROW did eventually arrive, and the next day, and the day after that, but Big M was not wagging his bushy tail as he had promised, slobbering happily over one and all. No running around or jumping up for him. No chasing his tail or digging in the garden burying bones. No tricks. No treats. All he could manage was to growl now and again at the poor harried woman, his wife, who fussed over him. Attired in a rumpled robe of purple and green stripes, stretched out on the couch in front of the TV, his oatmeal face grubby with a three-day growth of beard, sighing and moaning, but not doing anything she suggested that might make him feel any better. Like eating some chicken soup. Like making an appointment with the doctor. Like allowing her to call the doctor for him if he felt too ill to do it on his own.

"Nag, nag, nag," he barked irritably. "Women were put on this earth to nag."

He was resisting only out of habit, attempting to reclaim the infinitesimal iota of his masculine dignity, which never did allow him to call a doctor for each and every insignificant ailment. He couldn't remember ever having to take a day off from work because of illness, suffering stoically through the sniffles, the sore throat, the hacking cough, the heated temples indicating a low fever, more interested in preserving his image of stoic endurance than keeping the infection to himself. But this was different. A cosmic fear was beginning to creep uninvited into the convolutions of his brain. What if there really was something seriously wrong with him? He was the right age for it. Late forties to mid-fifties, when the first signs of rust and decay began to accumulate, despite regular care and maintenance. And he'd been getting careless lately, too comfortable in the daily routine, thinking things would remain the same forever. Obviously this was not an ordinary ailment, or else he would be more like himself by now. Wagging his tail, however feebly.

"Maybe you've been lying around too much. Sleeping all day. Awake all night with the TV blaring. No fresh air. I'd feel sick myself cooped up in here day after day," Emily remarked, returning from work. Full of energy. Plumping up his pillows.

"Nag, nag, nag," he repeated, more viciously this time, baring his teeth.

Unfazed by the threat, she continued on. "Why don't you try to get up and take a shower? Put some clothes on. Shave. You might be surprised at how much better you'd feel."

That did it! Awkwardly he raised himself into a sitting position, picked up the half-filled glass of stale ginger ale she had forced upon him earlier and slammed it down hard on the table. Luckily the glass didn't break, but the remaining liquid splattered far and wide.

Taken aback, Emily stared at this stranger who glowered at her from a face full of menace. This was not the man she married!

"For godsakes, M," she said, finally angry herself. "Look at the mess you've made."

"Look at the mess. Look at the mess," he mimicked. "Is that all you care about, having things neat and tidy?"

He did get up then, on weak lubberly legs, straightened his purple-striped robe around himself like royalty about to embark upon a great battle – whose loyal subjects had suddenly deserted him – and took the whole mess into the bathroom. All right then, if that's what she wanted. To preserve domestic harmony, he would suffer the discomfort of making himself more presentable. His irritation returning, he left the toilet seat up and the stubs of his beard peppering the sink in manly protest, *WHAT RIGHT HAD SHE…* until his superego asserted itself and he started to feel genuinely ashamed of his infantile behaviour.

Em, his loving wife. Trying her best to take care of him, to comfort him. It wasn't her fault he was dying, and the shower did make him feel better. But when he emerged clean and shaven to see her still wiping up the mess he had made, that down-trodden, put-upon, long-suffering, wifely expression on her face, walking to the sink to rinse out the cloth with her ass dragging along behind her as if bearing the totality of his disgrace in her polyester pants, he wanted to smack her hard right in the kisser.

"I'm sorry," he said instead.

Her shoulders relaxed then and she sat down on the sofa beside him.

"I worry about you, you know," she sniffled, the tears close to the surface now, a high water table inside his wife, the little m. Sensitive. That's what he liked about her from the first, her immediate and true feelings on full display, her empathy for the underdog. Working with troubled kids, resuming her career as a school counselor after their youngest started middle school, her heartfelt joy at their small successes, telling him about it at night, how the child really felt proud of himself, maybe for the first time in his life, you should have seen his face light up. Her own tears flowing.

He took her in his arms, his Emily, all their long years together enveloping the moment. M & m.

"I don't know what's the matter with me." Feeling like he was repeating some hackneyed words he had heard many times before, on some soap opera perhaps. "I feel so...annoyed...so...empty...so...depressed. Exhausted. I'm sorry. And I shouldn't be taking it out on you. I'll make an appointment with the doctor tomorrow. I promise."

But later, when the telephone woke him from his nap and he turned down the volume on the TV to hear what she was saying, he felt like snarling at her once again. Who was she talking to anyway, revealing his private indisposition to the world? Her words redefining his image. Who was she telling? Her mother? Their sons? Or some neighbour snooping into his business, ready to spread the news around the suburban sprawl: *You know that pudgy guy on Maple Street, number 125, with the two sons, gone now, works for the city, the one with the moustache and that ridiculous down-filled chrome-blue greatcoat his wife hates? Yes, that's the one. He's mental, you know. Nervous breakdown. Won't leave the house anymore. Lies in bed all day and stays up all night. It's his heart, actually, but he won't admit it. Blames everyone except himself for his misfortunes.*

"You have an enormous gob, you know, Emily," he informed her when she got off the phone. "It's no one else's business but our own what goes on in this house."

She just looked at him then, steely-eyed, as she brought over the bottle of extra-strength Tylenol and a plastic cup filled with water. "You better take a few of these," she said, "before you come to bed."

6

THE next morning, he was in for another annoyance. Instead of a person, he got a machine: *If you wish to make an appointment, press 1; if you wish to cancel an appointment, press 2; if this is an emergency, press 3; if you wish to speak to a receptionist, press 4.*

He pressed 4 and the same nasally enhanced whine said, "Dr. Malick's office. How can I help you?"

"I must have the wrong number," he said. "Sorry."

Steeling himself to try again, he got the same result. "I'm trying to reach Dr. Abrams," he complained.

"Dr. Abrams is no longer with us. You must have received our notice some time ago if you're an established patient."

Emmanuel was too taken aback to reply. After a slight pause, the voice continued: "What was your name again? Hello? Are you there? Would you like to make an appointment? What seems to be the trouble?"

"Yes. No. I don't know."

"I can't fit you in until next Thursday at two-fifteen. In case of emergency you can go to Outpatients at your local hospital."

"No. Yes. That's all right," he stammered.

"Name?"

Signing himself up then to be interrogated, examined, judged and sentenced by an unknown advocate. Out of habit, like the responsible suburban citizen he used to be, he marked it down on the calendar, though it was still possible to rebel and refuse to go. Where was Dr. Abrams, then? He had delivered both the boys. Chatting easily with Emmanuel as they waited together for the head to emerge, identically garbed in green cotton lab coats and masks. A man's man. Calmed him down. Made him feel necessary, as though he was helping. Afterward Emily had taken the children to a pediatrician and none of them had been back to Dr. Abrams for years. A nice fatherly type.

Emmanuel wouldn't have minded a civilized conversation with the old guy: *How are the boys? And the wife? Good weather we're having for February. Some times yet though, before it's all over, ha ha.* They could discuss his symptoms like gentlemen: *What seems to be the trouble then, young man? Not much really. Ennui. A lack of focus. Can't sleep. The little woman worrying. To tell the truth, that's why I'm here. Maybe you could prescribe something just to make her happy and I won't take up any more of your time.* Dr. Abrams clucking as he writes. *Yes, you've got a good wife there in Emily. Worries about you. Here you are. That should take care of it.* Shaking hands then. *Always nice to see a healthy young chap like yourself, Emmanuel. Hope not to see you again for another few decades, ha ha.*

When Emily came home from work, he was riled up, had something to say. "I called the doctor today," he barked.

"Good for you," she replied in her counselling voice and he felt hairs bristle on the back of his neck, his forelegs straighten, his tail stiffen up, ready for a fight. Who was she to patronize him?

"So where's Dr. Abrams gone?"

"Dr. Abrams?" she laughed. "Good Lord, M, the man retired ten years ago. Died shortly after. Just goes to show how healthy you've been." Smelling of the outdoors again, carrying with her the life energy he was missing. He was beginning to dislike her immensely.

"Well, I made an appointment. They can't get me in until next Thursday. With his replacement. A Dr. Malick. I hope that pleases you."

"Great!" she said, giving him a funny little smile, a victorious look he didn't appreciate.

But he controlled himself. He had done what she asked. Despite his own convictions, his own doubts and prejudices, his own beliefs, he was going along with the wishes of the little woman, and lord help her if she was wrong.

Lying on the couch, snarling behind her back as she prepared dinner, he made up his mind not to explain himself any longer to anyone.

7

NOT wanting to be late, he arrived early. Waiting room full. Every eye focused on the back of his hot and prickly neck as he gave his name.

Some sort of emergency at hospital. An unexpected delivery. "I'm afraid you'll have a bit of a wait," the receptionist apologized. "If you want to come back later?" She raised her eyebrows at him, but before he could formulate an answer, had already turned her attention elsewhere.

Feebly, he shook his head. After freeing himself of his down-filled coat and depositing it upon a rack by the door, a bright blue banner among the multitude of drab items already hanging there, he had no energy left for anything more demanding than just to sit.

As he squeezed himself into an unoccupied seat between two elderly women who reluctantly accommodated his bulk, he perceived an unmistakable aura of disapproval from all the other supplicants gathered here. Making negative judgements, he surmised. *What could possibly ail a middle-aged man of such robust proportions with his bristly reddish moustache and rosy cheeks, so unlike that sallow and cadaverous fellow over there in the corner? Heart* maybe? Cancer? *There was definitely a guilty look about him. A sexual deviant possibly, raised up in the seventies? Hepatitis? AIDS?*

Most of the patients were women, eyeing him through down-turned lashes, not bold enough to be caught staring. Self-consciously, he examined the pile of bedraggled magazines on the table beside him, selecting a few issues of *Time* of historical value. Possibly he missed something newsworthy when he was busy being younger.

As the disruption of his entrance diminished, the attention of the group returned to the two star performers hunkered on the floor in the corner of the room.

"What colour is that there, munchkin?" the mom asked, pointing to a large poster of the major organs of the human body tacked up on the waiting room wall. The sixty-four-thousand-dollar question! "Pink, did you say? That's RIGHT!" she shouted, glancing around at the audience, beaming for applause.

Another single parent, most likely, he reflected, consulting the doctor for each and every imaginary ailment just to have someone else take an interest. A few of the more elderly women did smile their encouragement. Longing for grandchildren, no doubt. Practicing their role.

The kid must have noticed him looking as he got up off the floor to toddle over, placing a grubby hand on his knee and gawking up into his face. Green goo dangling from both nostrils over red chapped lips directly into the open mouth. For awhile just staring silently as if to take account, then loudly snuffling the snot back into his nose.

"What's *your* name?" he asked.

Emmanuel buried his attention more deeply into a

rehashing of the Michael Jackson trial, but the kid wasn't old enough to take the hint.

"What's your *name*?" he demanded again, much more adamantly this time.

The entire congregation was attentive now, waiting for the answer.

Had it come to this? Was he to be humiliated by a two-year-old? There was silence. An interminably long pause. What should he say? Quickly he glanced around at the expectant faces.

Mr. Taggart?

Or maybe more informally, *Emmanuel?*

Surely not *Big M*. Not in front of all these strangers.

None of your business, kid. Go away. Go wipe your nose. Don't suck it up like that and swallow it for godsake. Hasn't your mother taught you the basic principles of good hygiene, or any manners, for that matter, you little brat?

At last the answer came to him and for that he was truly grateful. "What's yours?" he asked.

"Tommy!" the boy announced proudly.

There was a release, a collective sigh of approval as the child ran happily back to his mother, who was squatting on the dirty industrial grey-carpeted floor with a tissue ready.

"Blow," she crowed. "Blow hard now. That's a good boy."

Emmanuel almost expected to hear clapping from the audience, but the ladies restrained themselves to a smattering of genteel laughter instead. Cute. He probably should still take the receptionist's advice and go somewhere else, anywhere, for an hour or so. A few more people had come in, however, and he was afraid to lose his place in line.

After interminable eons of waiting, finally a name called out. There was a collective release, an audible shifting like at the end of a symphonic movement when no one was supposed to make much of an uproar, but some discreet coughing was expected. The doctor must have resolved the emergency at hospital and was ready now to meet patients.

Emmanuel closed the magazine and fanned himself. Hot flashes. He was the proper age for it. At least eight more people still ahead of him. He shut his eyes, but was afraid he might actually fall asleep in the stuffy room. Head falling back, mouth wide open, snoring. *Look, Mommy,* Tommy pointing, *look at the funny man, Mommy.* Moseying up to take a peek down his throat. The mother tittering, *shh, shh.* Giggles all around. An extra loud intake of breath. Jerking awake. Confused. Looking around. *Where am I?* Adding more fodder to the amusement of the onlookers. Better read some more instead. About the War. The Election. Vaguely remembered atrocities and half-forgotten scandals. Another name called. Goddamn! Why had he let Emily talk him into this? Too embarrassed to make a scene now and walk out.

Then he heard it – "Emmanuel?" – and they all stared at him again, snickering, he knew, like the kids in his class when they moved and he had to go to a new school in the middle of his Grade 4 year. It was then he first became aware of himself as an entity apart from others, introduced as the new kid. *Emmanuel, God is with us.* Whatever did he do to deserve a name like that? Some crazy notion of his mother's no doubt. A stigma for her only son to carry with him all his life.

He clambered to his feet, his ass numb, his foot

asleep, clumsily following a crisp woman to the inner recesses. There he was asked to undress and then waited some more in a small office by himself, attired in a pastel Johnny-shirt, hairy legs sticking out, barely decent, studying a poster labelled *Diseases of the Digestive System*, and in desperate boredom, skimming through a pamphlet about menopause.

Another woman entered. A nurse, he supposed. A young thing. Skinny with long curls.

"What seems to be the trouble then, Emmanuel?"

Don't know exactly. Not feeling right. Weak. Tired. Irritable. Can't think. Can't eat. Can't sleep. It's nothing really. The Wife insisted he make the appointment.

Height? Weight? Blood Pressure? Heart and lungs?

Listening through the stethoscope anterior and dorsal.

"Breathe deeply now. Cough."

Checking the reflexes.

Putting on a rubber glove.

"This might be a bit uncomfortable, but it's the best way we know how to check the prostate."

Stricken dumb then, the Big M. Paralysed. Unable to protest. Manhandled by this mere slip of a girl. Dr. Malick! He recalled that funny little smile on Emily's face. She knew. She knew and hadn't told him. She had allowed this profound humiliation to descend upon her husband of twenty-four years without the slightest warning. She would pay for it. Forever.

"You can get dressed now, Emmanuel," Dr. Malick said, and he could tell by the way she said it that she was smiling too, beneath her practiced stoic professional manner, laughing at his discomfiture in the depths of her girlish heart.

Women. Women. He had surrounded himself with women, he fumed, driving home. Driving fast, his foot heavy on the gas pedal, asserting his masculinity, squealing the tires. They swarmed around him like bees: his wife, his secretary, his sister calling from Florida to complain about his mother. And now this Dr. Malick. He had stepped into a nest of women in there, reading a book about menopause, intending to joke about it with the doctor until he turned out to be a woman.

Things had been different when the boys were still home. His manful presence was appreciated then. Games at the school, rooting for the team together with other fathers. *Is that your boy made the goal? He's not too bad, no he's not.* Buying sports equipment, the best, the most expensive sneakers. The father's opinion, the father's influence, the pillar of the family. *Hey, everybody, Dad's home!* In the summer, baseball games, golf with men from the office, stopping off for a beer after. Anorexic Dr. Malick *tsk-tsking* about his weight. He should have joined the gym when some of the younger guys were talking about it. Taken off a few pounds. Sweating and farting together. Manly pursuits.

When Emily arrived home from work, he was sitting in silence in the semi-dark living room with a glass of whiskey.

"What did the doctor say?" she asked, alarmed, flipping on the overhead light, rushing over to take a closer look without removing her coat. Scrutinizing his morose face, her hand on his arm.

"You didn't tell me he was a woman."

An almost imperceptible snort from the little m, her eyes filling up with suppressed mirth.

"You laugh." He glowered at her. "You knew all

along. You deliberately allowed me to be thoroughly humiliated."

The laughter did come forth then, bursting out, ripping the seams, spluttering uncontrollably through the air, tears streaming down his wife's convulsed face. "O, M," she managed through the hilarity, biting on her upper lip as she took note of his stony expression.

"I'm glad you find this so amusing," he remarked bitterly.

That brought her up short. "What did Dr. Malick say was wrong with you?" she asked, serious now, putting her hand on his arm again.

"Nothing," he said. "Absolutely nothing. She could find nothing wrong with me. I sat in that stinking waiting room with a bunch of yakking women and their snot-nosed kids for two hours. TWO HOURS. Your Dr. Malick finally looks me over for a few minutes and pronounces me a healthy specimen. Examined every hole," he mumbled, revealing to her the depths of his embarrassment, taking a big slurp of Jack Daniels to wash it down.

He knew without looking that her face was turning bright red with strain, her laughter so near the surface that her eyes were bulging and her cheeks puffed out.

"O, M," she repeated. Got up then to take off her coat and giggle in private.

When she returned with a drink for herself, she had regained control. "I knew if I told you, you wouldn't go," she said in the reasonable tones of an adult, explaining the difficulties of life to a recalcitrant child. "And I was worried about you. You've always been so healthy, full of energy, easygoing." She sat down next to him and soothed his ruffled feathers with gentle fingers.

"She wants me to get a blood test as soon as possible. She said forty-five was a dangerous age. She said she would refer me to a specialist if the test didn't show up anything specific. She said my blood pressure was a bit high. And no wonder, the strain I was under."

He was able to look at her now and let go of his anger, to see the humour of his predicament though he wasn't about to let her know that. He just allowed her an indulgent smile as she went into the kitchen to prepare his dinner.

8

HE still couldn't eat much, forced himself to chew a couple of bites, the steak rare the way he liked it, oozing blood onto his plate, baked potato heavily topped with sour cream, a crisp green salad shining Italian dressing, garlic bread greasy with butter. She went to a lot of trouble, his Emily, to prepare a nice meal for him, but all he could do was nibble at the edges to show his appreciation.

With the arrogance of the healthy, Emmanuel tended to look upon illness as either a product of personal weakness or of old age, taking for granted all those well-functioning natural systems that performed their tasks so efficiently day after day – digesting, processing, eliminating, transmitting, pumping – without any personal advice or interference from him. But Dr. Malick surely wouldn't request blood tests unless she suspected something more serious than just a common flu. She would have written out a prescription for some sort of antibiotic and that would be the end of it.

Reflecting back, he now realized that there may have been some indications all along, that he had preferred to ignore. Foreshadowings. Like a heavy fogbank over the ocean, barely visible from a sunny shore. *Not as young as I used to be, heh heh*, he joked, a pain in his knee, an ache in the lower back, an occasional twinge in the neck, an abnormal sluggishness of the bowels. Increasingly restless, bored, irritable and out of sorts, though attempting to maintain a show of his usual good humour, whistling while he worked. Until it had all come crashing down on him and he finally saw his life for what it really was – a meaningless pretence.

It was indeed possible that a secretive, malignant, terminal disease was even now in the process of murdering him slowly. A short easy life and a long and horrifying death, contrary to his mother's hopeful prognostications. First he'd need a cane to get around, then a wheelchair, until he could no longer get up at all, his final days spent staring at the ceiling with a tube up his nose and some stranger occasionally coming in to change his diaper.

Or perhaps a surprise attack when he least expected it. On the crowded sidewalk, a spectacle, suddenly falling over clutching his chest. Behind the wheel of his car, careening out of control on the highway, heroically avoiding the oncoming traffic to smash into the abutment.

Or all alone in their bedroom, taking his last painful breaths, Emily coming home to find him gone. Gone like John.

He put his hand to his left breast, eyeing the great mound of food still left on his plate with revulsion, following the goblets of grease as they passed down the esophagus and through his digestive system to deposit themselves snugly around the arteries of his heart.

Like father like son. *Forty-five is a dangerous age*, she had told him.

"What's wrong?" Emily asked, her brow wrinkled with concern.

"I don't know. I don't know," he said, real despair in his voice now.

"She's thorough. She wants to make sure. It's just routine," Emily reassured him.

But who can let go of the primal fear that lurks in the dark corner of everyone's mind? Most people try to ignore it, acquiescing to the discomfort of medical testing merely as a safety precaution. Just to make sure. One's blood and excretions minutely analyzed. The cardiogram, the mammogram, the ultrasound, the barium enema, the colonoscopy. Routine procedures everyone feels they must endure. For the same reason you buy insurance. No one really expects things to turn out badly.

What? Not me, doc. I'm barely past middle age. There must be some mistake!

It's the price we pay for being alive, my son. It can happen to anyone.

At the laboratory, the line moving fast, victims herded efficiently through, each clutching a stub of paper with a number.

Emmanuel Taggart, Number 82, watched, fascinated, as two glass vials filled up quickly with his own bright red blood. He expected it to be pallid, as it had appeared under his lower eyelid that morning when he pulled down the skin to examine the hue in the bathroom mirror. A sickly pale yellow with only a narrow rim of red. Definitely anemic, he diagnosed himself, the corpuscles losing their vigour, their stamina, tired of the same old routine, hauling in food and dumping out waste products, circulating around and around day after day. So he was surprised to see that it looked quite normal, like regular blood, identical to all the other vials lined up in racks, neatly identified with small white labels. The technician taped a piece of cotton to his arm and shouted for Number 83, a portly man with his shirtsleeve rolled up, his ruddy face proclaiming high blood pressure.

For some time afterwards, Emmanuel sat behind the wheel of his car in the dimly lit underground parking lot contemplating his options. What if? What if, indeed, his disease, whatever it was, turned out to be terminal? Old Dr. Abrams putting a kindly arm around his shoulder. *You've only got a few months, my son. Sorry.* He bit down hard on his lower lip. It wouldn't do to start *boo-hoo-hooing* in a public place, a grown man like him. People were already taking notice, he realized now, women passing by with quick little steps, clutching their purses, searching with panicked fingers for their vial of mace, their whistle, their pepper spray, in case this man was some sort of pervert.

There were few places left in the world where one could just sit and think without attracting undue attentions: in waiting rooms, but only if you had an appointment; on benches in malls while the wife finished her shopping; in the park, maybe for a short while, preferably with a bag of lunch or some chunks of stale bread for the ducks. One was expected to be busy, to be always hurrying somewhere, to be doing something. Loitering was strictly forbidden and sitting anywhere for an undue length of time was looked upon as definitely suspicious. Terrorists were lurking everywhere.

It was too early to go home and park himself in front of the TV to doze while listening to the loonies on the afternoon talk shows. There was nowhere he could go to get away from the terror of his own mortality. Suffering and pain. Disability and death. Tossing and turning in the middle of the night, soaked in sweat, zooming in on aches and pains he had ignored for years. Searching his decaying flesh for lumps and moles. *Look at this, Em! Was that there before? It definitely seems to be expanding.* Pacing the floor, bug-eyed in the darkness. Comatose at the first light of dawn.

Perhaps he should pop into the office to prove to them that he was alive, though still waiting for the verdict to find out if he had a future. Hard not knowing, but he was doing his best.

Chin up, old man. We're all under the same threat of extinction, after all.

"Well, if it isn't the man himself," Rose chirped. "What brings you out on a cold day like this, Mr. Taggart? Think we can't handle things on our own around here, ha ha?"

She backed up to take a good look at him and shook her head. "So what's the doctor say is wrong widdja?"

"No diagnosis yet. Behold the Great Mystery," he lamely joked.

"No kidding?" she remarked, afraid to say anything more. There were things people didn't mention out loud. Like the dreaded C word, for instance.

They stood for a prolonged moment in uncomfortable silence. What had he come here for? He had pushed all his papers into Rose's capable hands when he left the office two weeks ago. She could take care of everything. He was no longer needed, filling up space, guarding his own importance in a small room containing a large desk behind a door labelled MR. TAGGART.

"Thank you, Rose," he said and meant it, holding her by the shoulders, wanting to kiss the top of her white part, the flakes of dandruff. Rose, his beleaguered secretary, always willing to do more than her share to help out, scurrying here and there like a little squirrel, her cheeks puffed out with kindness. *I'll take care of it. I'll help. Can I do something for you? I'll get it. Please, somebody, why don't you want me, what's wrong with me, why am I all alone in the world with two teenaged children to support, even though I've done the best I could my entire life?* Rose. He wished he could comfort her, hug her, but he didn't dare. The management had established strict policies concerning sexual harassment. There had been pamphlets and directives defining every possible scenario.

Down the empty highway, driving home, Emmanuel purposely missed his exit, the cruise control forcing him onward, out of the suburbs into the country, the scrubby clumps of forest he dimly remembered. Was it Exit 17 he took that evening? He couldn't say for sure. Everything looked slightly familiar, but different too, in the bright sunlight of mid-afternoon. He turned off anyway, on Exit 17 to Deep River. Took a left. Didn't recall the traffic light being there, and there seemed to be too many houses, nestled in clumps of cultivation. He must have the wrong number.

After a while, he gave up and went back to the highway. What was he doing out here anyway? If he did find her house, would he dare knock on her door to apologize, to make things right, to explain himself? He had tried hard all his life not to make mistakes. *Mistakes haunt you until you die*, his father told him gravely. What crimes had the old man committed to encumber him with such a burden of guilt? He never said, and it didn't seem appropriate to ask, even if Emmanuel had been able to stand back from his own preoccupations long enough to consider his father's existence. Now, of course, it was too late.

It was important to clarify one's behaviour to those left behind so that they would not judge harshly, Emmanuel philosophized.

Look, he would say to her, *it was all a big misunderstanding and I really did appreciate the meal. I liked your dog, Deal, and your little girls, Penny and Sara, and you too, actually, heh heh. What did you say your name was?*

And she would say, *Santa! How nice of you to come back. Did you bring your sack this time?*

9

EMILY speaking in metaphors, sipping from a glass of red wine.

"Like plants we germinate, we bloom, then we die. Some of us flower early in spring, some blossom all summer long, some not until late in the season. Human beings are no different. M, are you listening? Except that our sizeable brain and our opposing thumb enable us to produce more than offspring. We can create, discover, change the world for better or for worse. It all depends on how much life energy we possess. Disease attacks those who have lost their life energy. You have to bring it back, M. What I mean is, you've got to get yourself up and doing, to find something that interests you, to get a hobby, to get yourself involved. You may just be a late bloomer, M. Your true flowering may still be ahead of you. One never knows what the future holds. Anyhoo, you can't just lie there like a lump and expect to get better. M? Are you listening, M?"

Emmanuel, dozing on the davenport, woke up to the silence when she stopped talking.

He didn't get too excited about these philosophical ruminations his wife was prone to. Ever since she got back in the workforce advising kids what to do with their lives, she thought she had all the answers. He tended to lose track of her pontifications early on, so he could never appreciate the conclusions. His own thinking had always been more to the point. *Say what you mean. And mean what you say,* he had advised his boys.

Emily was literary. Full of allusions and similes, reflecting upon the symbolism of this or that. Reading a book while he watched TV. Fiction.

"Why bother to read something someone made up," he told her, "when there's an information explosion out there. If you open a book, you should be able to learn something useful."

"You learn about life," she argued. "You get to know how other people think. You learn tolerance and understanding."

"Lies, lies," he countered, "all lies. It gets you into deep trouble when you believe you know how other people think. No one ever knows what anyone else is really thinking."

But Emily had spent her life trying to understand others. Analyzing motives, thinking positively, striving to bring out the best in everyone, her heart filled with patience and love.

When they first met, he felt immediately that he could trust her with his weaknesses, knowing she would not dismiss his strengths because of them. He had found a home in her, a resting place, her hand fitting neatly into his, the rhythm of their steps moving naturally together. That's not to say it was purely a rational decision. Even now he felt a quickening in his body when he recalled the early years. The wisps of dark hair along the graceful curve of her neck, golden eyes hidden by long lashes, soft fingers stroking his body, small perfectly formed breasts, the intensity of her passion, the smell of the outdoors always about her. How compliant she was, how loving, with her hair undone in loose waves around her shoulders, washing his feet and bending over to dry them with her long hair like Mary Magdalene, fulfilling his adolescent fantasy formed when he suffered through Sunday school in obedience to his mother.

Emily. His Emily.

As he looked across the room at a plump little woman with a puffy blond hairdo, her bifocals halfway down her nose, reading in the big armchair with her feet tucked up underneath, he could almost still see her within this other person.

She must have felt him staring for she glanced up from the book. "M?" she said.

"I love you, you know," he croaked through the lump in his throat, slightly embarrassed to be speaking the hackneyed words that came so easily to others.

She got up then and came to sit beside him, kissed him on his forehead and cheeks, but his momentary desire had been mental only and he could give her no response. She was right. His life energy was lacking. The opposing thumb meant nothing to him.

"Can I get you anything?" finally she said. "Coffee? Tea? Hot milk? Ginger ale? A drink?"

The ringing of the telephone stopped her recitation. He turned down the TV so he could hear what she was saying.

It was Gerry, their oldest. Beginning work on his doctorate in English literature, taking on the inclinations of his mother. Turned into an artsy-fartsy type. Beard and long hair. Poetry and jazz. Even the way he spoke the most commonplace words had changed. Cultured now. Teaching introductory courses to first-year university students.

"Not himself lately," she said into the receiver, glancing over to where he lay, his eyes focused on the screen so she wouldn't think he was listening.

The words made him angry. He could feel prickles of rage stiffen his face and curl his fingers into fists. What right had she to judge him? And why did she have to open her big gob to tell the world? He could imagine her at work, in the Teachers' Room at recess. *My husband, he's not himself lately.* And the old biddies, they could let their imaginations run wild.

He pretended to be asleep until she went to bed, then got up from the couch to examine his image once again in the bathroom mirror. Striving for objectivity. Trying to catch himself unaware, as if by a stranger. A middle-aged man with a forthright, bristly moustache, slightly chubby still, but beginning to wane. He leaned in close to peer through the black tunnels of his eyes that led into his skull to see if he could discover anything there.

Not himself, she said. Where had he gone to then, if, indeed, he had ever been? A brief period in university of late-night, marijuana-induced discussions about the meaning of life, trying to find himself. But then finding Emily instead. His thoughts becoming preoccupied with worries regarding the mortgage and the importance of saving regularly for retirement and the children's education. Everything set out clearly before him, predetermined. All he had to do was to follow instructions.

The one-year-old, Emily read out loud from the book, *gets more dependent and more independent at the same time. Let him out of the playpen if he insists!*

Boys, she read, *need a friendly, accepting father. There's more about the father's relations with his children in Sections 503-504. Want me to read you those?*

It was all there in black and white, his duties and obligations as a good husband and father with his steady job, a new car every four years, a comfortable home in the suburbs. Vacationing for two weeks in the summer at a rented cottage by the sea until the boys no longer wanted to go. After they grew up and left, watching the world pass by on his 32-inch TV, hiding his discontent under a jolly red moustache, thinking his life was still ahead of him.

Now with downsizing and upgrading, it wouldn't be long before he was forced into early retirement. And what would he do then? His boys, young men now, busy with their own lives. Emily involved in her new career, old M left behind, no longer a contender, not even, so it now seemed, in the race at all. Bored, flaccid, a spectator, moping like a spoiled child whining about his own minor discomforts.

He had been satisfied with his life. He got all he ever wanted: a home, a family, a steady job. But it had evaporated somehow. Disappearing into a nostalgic past which could never be retrieved. The boys gone and his wife transformed, not the Emily she was. And Emmanuel, the Big M, a mere husk of what he used to be. Though he couldn't imagine himself actually dying, neither could he tolerate what he would become if he didn't. Decrepit. Old. Stepping off the curb supported by the walker. Stopping impatient traffic as painfully, slowly, he dragged himself over the crosswalk. Going nowhere.

Rage. Rage. Rage. In a juvenile rage, rebelling against everything that sustained him. Too old even now to stir up enough energy to make it real, the anger pique merely, the rebellion feeble whining, the mundane recitation of complaints listened to out of pity, before being dismissed and forgotten. *Go on now, Emmanuel. Lie down.* The old cur, foul-smelling and evil-tempered, allowed to spend the rest of his days on his mat in the basement. One doesn't actually kick him down the stairs, though one might have a mind to. *GO ON now. GO!*

Rummaging in the dresser drawer for the scissors. Clipping off the longer hairs of his moustache into the toilet bowl. Zapping the remainder with the electric razor. Considered doing the rest of his body as well, hairless as a newborn babe, but, reasonably, decided against it. People might think he truly was a cancer victim and he hadn't yet sunk so low as to use that kind of ploy for sympathy.

Without the moustache, he did look quite different. Or at least he didn't remember himself looking like that, the slightly swollen area below his nose immense, giving him a pugnacious appearance.

Don't mess with that man, Mama, he's no longer himself.

10

FINALLY a call from Dr. Malick's receptionist with the verdict: *We the jury find the defendant Emmanuel "M" Taggart guilty, definitely guilty. This man is no longer able to keep a stiff upper lip, to put his shoulder to the wheel and hang in there doing his share and bearing his load, holding his head high, smiling in the face of adversity, a pillar of the community, a solid support to his wife, a shining example to his children. They should have thrown away the mould after they made him.*

"The results of your blood work are in, Mr. Taggart. Dr. Malick would like to see you on Friday at 10 a.m."

He felt heat under his collar, loosened the neck of his robe. "What's wrong?" he asked, attempting a casual tone, jovial even, still able to force a smile in the face of adversity.

"I'm sorry, I can't give out that information," Miss Crisp announced.

So be it then, he acquiesced, bowing his head, the stiffness in his upper lip faltering under beads of sweat.

Heretofore from his presumed vantage point of relative youthfulness and good health, he had never been particularly afraid of death. It was, after all, an inevitable part of life. They would all die. Emily. His sons. United at last in the great horde of the unliving. Statistically speaking, he would be the first to go, in the faraway future when he could face his imminent demise with the wisdom and resignation of old age. But not yet! He wasn't nearly ready.

This time, the waiting room was empty, an intimation of doom. Emmanuel was ushered quickly into the inner sanctum where he had suffered such gross humiliation just the week before. Even in his convoluted state, he couldn't keep from noticing that Dr. Malick looked quite fetching in a soft lavender sweater, tight black skirt and sensible shoes, her long dark hair pulled back into a loose bun. Studying his file, as he patiently waited, nonchalantly clenching his molars.

"Well, Emmanuel." She smiled up at him. "I'm sorry to say we are unable to find anything definite wrong with you. Not so far, at any rate." Twinkling like a schoolgirl barely able to suppress her twitters.

He let his breath escape like stale air from a busted balloon.

"So," she said. "We refer to this kind of thing as an idiopathic disorder, which means that at the present time, you remain a medical mystery. How are you feeling now?"

"Better," he lied. "Relieved."

"Sleeping all right? Appetite good? No more mood swings? Energy level okay? Bowels and bladder normal?" she read from his file. "You look as though you've lost some weight...which is good," she smirked. "Let's weigh you."

"I still can't...function," he stammered. "I'm not myself."

She ignored this, marking down his statistics, taking his blood pressure. "I'll arrange an appointment for you with Dr. Acton. He's our specialist in Internal Medicine. But frankly, he's so booked up you probably won't get to see him until September at the earliest. And you say you are feeling better?"

Dumbly he nodded.

"Fine then," she said cheerfully, standing up to dismiss him. "If any new symptoms develop, just give us a call."

Feeling like a little boy sent back to his seat by the teacher, his problem not worthy enough to be considered, he made his way back to his car. A medical mystery. A pathetic idiot. Turned on the radio. Music to ease the soul. *You're over forty and not a young pup any more,* a brash and cocky voice announced, *BUT you can still be in the game. What you've given up in vigour, you've gained in wisdom.* Easy enough for him to say, but when would this promised wisdom come to him? Emmanuel pondered and missed hearing what he would have to buy to get back into the game. It seemed that the floor had dropped out from underneath him, leaving him exposed, belly-up, moaning and groaning to those passing by up above. He had to get a hold of things, dust himself off at least, and stand up like a man.

"Nothing," he told Emily when she called.

"Nothing?"

"Nothing."

"What is it then, Emmanuel?"

"I'm a medical mystery. According to your Dr. Malick, I've got pathetic idiot's disease."

Emily ignored his lame attempt at humour. "Well, that's a relief, anyway," she said. "Sort of."

But really, it wasn't. He would have preferred some sort of a diagnosis. Something he could speak about with dignity if anyone asked, retaining a modicum of masculine swagger: *It's just the old ticker; they do run down, you know.* Or, *They're considering a brain scan.* Or, *We're waiting for the biopsy, no sense getting all upset before we know for sure.* But now what could he say? Any sympathy he had received heretofore would soon turn to scorn. *That Emmanuel Taggart, the Big M, is just pretending to be sick, taking a prolonged vacation to sleep in, a shirker, a liar, a hypochondriac, making his long-suffering wife wait upon him while he lounges on the davenport, the lazy old lout, whining and complaining and watching trash on TV, expecting the whole world to feel sorry for him because he has lost his life energy and the waves in his brain have become ripples.*

"S.A.D.," Emily consoled him later.

"Sad?" he exploded. "Sad? What kind of a statement is that? Is this just a bad mood I'm indulging myself with in your humble medical opinion?"

"No, no," she explained patiently. "S. A. D. Seasonal Affective Disorder. It happens to people in February. Your hormones go out of whack because they lack sunlight."

"Harumph," he scoffed. "Up north they must only be normal six months of the year then. Honestly, Em, you shouldn't really believe all the garbage you read. They come up with these new labels constantly to justify themselves. *'When faced with a medical mystery, we just make up a new name for it.'* He tried to imitate the girlish voice of Dr. Malick, pursing his lips and bouncing his shoulders up and down.

Emily laughed, but he wasn't in the mood to see the humour in anything any longer, resuming his discontented harangue, muttering his disgust at the incompetence of the medical profession, the profiteering drug companies making millions off the decrepit flesh of the terminally ill and elderly, the decadence of the modern world in general, until it was obvious she was ignoring him, whereupon he gave her a withering look and turned up the volume on the TV so loud as to be irritating to pay her back for her inattentiveness.

The daily activities of his life had become like a swarm of early spring black flies, not biting yet, but exasperating him beyond measure. He didn't want her sympathy. He wanted to be left alone. She was constantly annoying him with her interference, making lists of medical resources: neurologists, psychiatrists, psychologists, therapists, counselors – "all sorts," the corner of her lip turning self-deprecatingly downward – chiropractors, healers, homeopaths, herbalists, naturopaths, medical intuitives.

"You could consult any one of these," she advised him. "Lots of people are. Medical science has diversified in the modern age. There's all sorts of help out there."

"There are all sorts of charlatans looking for new ways to bilk the gullible," he snarled.

"You've got to do something, M. It's been nearly a month now, and you're not any better."

She presented him with anecdotal evidence:

The music teacher at their school had a variety of undiagnosed medical problems until her dentist replaced her mercury fillings.

The principal was going to a Swedish masseuse regularly to relieve stress.

The Smithers, Lila and Ted, swore by their homeopath and took medication specially designed for their individual personalities, which bolstered their life force so their immune systems could more efficiently fight off disease.

She had even heard of someone rejuvenated by a therapist who massaged his energy field without touching his body at all.

"You've got to do something, M, for godsakes," she repeated. "We can't go on like this."

But his self-image had curdled and he looked upon the entire world with a soured eye.

"Is that what you gab about in the Teachers' Room? The medical problems of an aging population? I'm sure you've minutely analyzed your husband's present condition in the public forum. I wish, Emily, that you'd keep our private lives private."

"There's no talking to you these days, is there? You've become totally irrational." She got up and left him then, her angry, load-in-the-pants walk, and he fumed for a while, green clouds of toxic spite drifting out of the cavities of his head, until the canned laughter distracted him and he turned his attention back to the TV to see if he could get at least one chuckle out of prime time.

Later on, he felt ashamed once again. She was only trying to help him out of his miserable condition after all. But for some reason the full gamut of his emotions could only extend to shades of grey, seeming to prefer black over all. Fear, anger, despair, confusion, hatred, scorn, boredom, restlessness, guilt, and most of all, a deep and relentless disgust at his own forty-five-year-old person, past, present, and future. She was right. He had to do something. He couldn't lie here on this sofa forever. Things would either get worse or better and it was obvious the medical profession wasn't going to help a pathetic idiot like him.

11

THE resolution to do something fermented in his brain throughout a night of troubled sleep, and though he pretended otherwise, he was wide awake early in the morning, listening to Emily's preparations for the day. The slither of clothing, the clomp of feet going down the stairs, the clang of dishware. It was no wonder mankind saw little of the benevolent spirits and gods of the household for all the noise he made asserting his own importance.

When her car pulled out of the driveway, he rose up looking forward to a bright new day of good intentions to erase the mistakes of the past. Using the bit of energy still remaining, he showered, soaping himself vigorously to scrub away the accumulations of dead skin, scraped the stubble off the unfamiliar naked face he saw in the mirror, dressed himself informally in relaxed-fit jeans and sweater, donned his blue greatcoat and prepared to face the consequences of his former life.

As this was not to be a half-hearted fly-by-night gesture, but methodical, well-organized, immaculately recorded, scientifically oriented research, his first stop was at a nearby shopping centre to purchase the necessary equipment. *You've got to do something, M*, his wife had insisted, and she was right.

He would search until he found her.

If he had been tortured into an explanation of why this seemed so necessary, he wasn't sure he could convince his interlocutor that his reasons were justified, or even that his actions were in any way reasonable. But in the depths of his soul, he felt that his present condition had something to do with his disgraceful departure the evening his descent began. Sneaking out with his tail between his legs, baring his teeth to force the other dog into complicity, fleeing the premises after having consented to eat his fill. Shameful. *For shame, Emmanuel.*

But his mistakes did not have to haunt him forever. He could still redeem himself. When he found her, his life would return to normal. He would be himself again. And he was hopeful that if he took the time to do it, it could be done. This was not, after all, an epic quest for the Golden Fleece or the Ark of the Covenant. All he sought was a youngish blond woman who made homebrew and liked to cook. With two small daughters named Penny and Sara and a big dog named Deal. Who had known someone named John. But John was gone. Off the highway on Exit something or other. Out in the country. Maybe twenty kilometres or so to the left, definitely no more, a small white house on the right-hand side surrounded by forest. He was sure he'd recognize it, even though it was quite dark when he arrived there before.

That wasn't much to go on, yet he already felt a small sense of accomplishment, glancing down at the purchases set out neatly beside him on the front seat: a clipboard covered in black vinyl, a yellow legal-sized pad of lined paper, a good-quality, fluorescent-green ballpoint pen. The first day of school after summer vacation, the new book bag filled with the year's supplies: virginal scribblers, pencils sharpened to precise points the night before in a zippered case with a picture of Batman, bright blue notebook with five dividers, sixty-four crayons in a sturdy cardboard box, each still properly outfitted in its tube of paper and lined up by colour. Just for a moment there was magic in these things. An anticipation of the new year to come. The smell of promise. But by the time the bell rang for recess, hope had already dissipated, the pencil dulled, the eraser making black smudges and ruining the first page, a different teacher speaking the same hackneyed words about the same old rules, desks no longer lined up in straight rows on the freshly polished floor, students back to their habitual rowdy insolence.

When he approached the first exit past his own, he remembered to pull off to the shoulder of the highway and make a notation: MARCH 2, he printed neatly at the top of the page, EXIT 14 – SUMMERVILLE, DEXTER. Not that he expected to find anything here, in what was commonly referred to as "outer-suburbia." He was certain he drove a much greater distance that afternoon, his brain absenting itself to wherever, for who knows how long, and for whatever reason; but, determined as he was to conduct this search according to strict scientific principles, with orderly and precise record-keeping that left nothing to chance, he had to pursue all avenues methodically.

Clicking the odometer to zero. Taking a left at the stoplight. He would drive twenty-five kilometres as his plan directed. Not anticipating any significant results on this first day, he relaxed. A practice run merely. Farther on down the highway, tomorrow or the next day, he would put all his senses on alert.

This road was lined with well-kept houses, ranch-type, newer than in his own neighbourhood, all the rectangular boxes side by side, each containing its own sorrows. In the day-by-day routine of life, he was coming to realize, the brief moments of joy were as fleeting as water in a sieve; whereas the recollection of every misfortune, those already past and those yet to come, lingered like a bad odour in the air. *A long life and an easy death,* his mother had often sighed, *is the best one can hope for.*

Still vigorous in her seventies, she had outlived his father by more than twenty years and would most likely endure for twenty more. A tough old bird, his mother. In Florida, where she had purchased a duplex, forging out a new life for herself. Taking up painting landscapes as a hobby. Playing bridge. Always on the go. When Amanda too moved down south with husband and children in tow, his mother's cup of happiness was complete. Though she missed Emmanuel of course, she would complain whenever he called, and hadn't seen enough of Gerry and Mike now that they were grown. The last time they had visited two years ago, it was just Emily and himself. During March break. He hated the traffic, the heat, the tittle-tattle of women, the endless shopping, the strain of remaining good-natured on holiday. Played golf once with his brother-in-law. Glad to get back home, to the fresh air, to the cool night breezes, away from the air-conditioned world of elderly charm. On the plane, looking down at the suburban sprawl, like a cancer spread along the entire eastern seaboard.

12

REFLECTING thus about the hopelessness of mankind, he let his attention wander from the business at hand and didn't notice the car ahead slowing down for a left turn until it was too late. Pulling the wheel hard in a valiant attempt to avoid a collision, he veered toward the sidewalk. Squeal of tires before the jolt, the sickening discordance of breaking glass and crumpling metal. A done deed. An irreversible moment. *Jesus Christ. Goddamn.* Good thing he had been dawdling, going slow, regarding the landscape. Wiping his hands through his thinning hair, he had the presence of mind to flick on the emergency lights, stopped thus in the middle of the pavement, before getting out of the car to face the consequences.

The other driver was not moving, hunched over the wheel. Good God! There couldn't possibly be an injury! It was merely a fender bender, a slight nudge, a momentary inattentiveness. Emmanuel hurrying now, the adrenalin pumping through his system, knuckling the window, *ARE YOU ALL RIGHT IN THERE?* Peering in at a stocking cap, a muffler. Opening the door. The figure moving then. Hitting the steering wheel hard with a mittened fist. An old fellow.

"*KURAT VÕTTAKS!*" the man shouted, looking up at Emmanuel with bright blue eyes half hidden in hummocks of transparent flesh. He grinned broadly, displaying sparse yellowed teeth in a face as smooth and pink as a baby's. "Cannot get away with anything anymore!"

"Are you all right?" Emmanuel inquired. "So sorry."

"Yes, yes, I am all right. Please forgive me," he said with a heavy continental accent. "I seem to revert to the mother tongue under stress. What is the damage?"

Slowly he unfolded himself from the car, Emmanuel offering his arm as they shuffled together to the scene of the crime.

"I am not seeing anything wrong here," he said, examining the rear bumper. "You, mister, are not so lucky."

A broken headlight, a crunched fender, pieces of glass scattered over the road.

"Juhan Lipp," he introduced himself, extending his hand. "I am known as John in this country."

John? John is gone. A fleeting, ridiculous thought. There must be thousands, millions of Johns in the world. "Emmanuel Taggart," he replied. "So sorry," he apologized again.

"You might know," Juhan said. "The first time I have been able to drive out in weeks, and this will happen. I almost made it to my home too. That is where I live, right over there." He motioned with his chin. "We will keep this incident our little secret, shall we? I am pulling into the garage. There should be a broom and a dustpan somewhere in there. You, perhaps, could sweep up the evidence?"

As Emmanuel swept, the old man talked. "I am not supposed to be driving, you see. I am not able to afford it any longer. The insurance company keeps raising my rates. If I get much older I will have to be a millionaire," he chuckled. "Besides, she does not want me to use her car. Anna." He lingered slightly over the name, his eyes softening, a trace of a smile lifting the corners of his lips, even as he continued to complain. "My daughter, Anna. A hard taskmaster. A mathematician. She is a firm believer in right and wrong, in truth and consequences. She is at a conference today. She took a ride and I am a man who does not pass an opportunity by when it happens my way. I was only driving a few miles to the store to buy cigarettes. She does not allow me a smoke either. I have to work hard for my vices." He chuckled again. "Maybe you could pull your car into the driveway? In case someone comes."

Emmanuel felt immense relief and gratitude. It could have been worse, it could have been so much worse. He was the one getting away with something. The old man obviously didn't want the accident reported. Now all he had to worry about was getting his own car repaired before Emily saw it. Might as well avoid long explanations of what he had been up to, when she imagined him safely tucked under the covers still in bed, or at least prone on their davenport watching TV, recuperating from his mysterious illness. Explanations that might be misunderstood. Words that could go awry. Arguments that might ensue. Wasn't she the one who had told him he had to do something, that he could no longer go on this way? Well, he was doing it. The assertive mode taking hold, he took control of this present situation.

"Why don't we go someplace where I can buy you a cup of coffee?" he suggested. "It's the least I can do."

"I would not mind. I am not to smoke in the house. She has strict rules about everything. I am not supposed to drink coffee either. There is a Tim Hortons by the highway. Smoke-free," Juhan said ruefully. "Down the other way there is a little Mom and Pop place not too far from here."

At the restaurant Juhan lit up.

"It is the only thing I have left to make me feel like I am still a man," he justified himself. "After my wife died, Anna insisted I move in with her. I do get these spells from time to time. Senior moments, I believe they are called. But it certainly does get boring out here in greater suburbia. I cannot do much any more. Sit, lie down, and scratch myself, like an old flea-bitten dog. Do you live around here?"

"No, actually. I'm just passing through looking for a woman."

Juhan raised a quirky eyebrow. With his thick shock of dishevelled white hair poking up at odd angles after he removed his woolly cap, he resembled an ancient gnome from the old country. "If that is what you are after, you have come to the wrong place, young man. There are no women in Summerville," he said. "No available ones, at any rate, that I know of. Except for Anna, my daughter..." Scrutinizing him closely now, blowing smoke out of both hairy nostrils. "Too old for you maybe, I figure."

"No. No. No. No. I'm married," Emmanuel explained.

"Oh?" Both eyebrows raised up this time. "I see."

"What I mean is, I'm on a search. A mission. A quest, if you will. I'm looking for this one particular woman."

The eyebrows elevated, the clear blue gaze remaining fixed upon his face, Emmanuel, having said that much, had no recourse but to elaborate, relating the unexpected journey that led to his shameful and ridiculous descent and his newly formed plan to redeem himself.

"So," said Juhan when he finished, "the reason you want to find this woman is to apologize?"

Suddenly he wasn't so sure anymore. He had lost direction, his yellow pad empty except for the exit number and the date. What exactly did he want?

"Now I am an old fogey, right?" Juhan continued. "But there is a thing or two left over I still know. What you are looking for is—" A severe coughing fit overtook him, deep heavy spasms, watering his eyes and making further conversation impossible.

"Maybe I should quit," he finally spluttered, wiping his pink face with a paper serviette.

As Emmanuel dropped the old man off at his house, feeling a sudden and inexplicable sense of loss at the parting, the words came from his mouth before he had a chance to think about what he was saying and to consider the ramifications.

"Look John," he said. "Why don't you come with me on the search? I'll pick you up in the mornings and we'll do the exits." Reaching into the back seat, he showed the old man his clipboard, his pad. "What's your number? I'll call you. We'll sneak out together during the week when our women are working. Waddja say?"

The two conspirators grinned at each other and shook hands over the deal. For the first time in three weeks Emmanuel felt a spark of his old energy returning. The road of life stretched out before him with its unpredictable twists and turns, the possibility of something new around every corner, unexpected disruptions in the usual routine. Good or bad? It all depended on how one looked at it.

Driving back home with something to look forward

to. Stopping at a garage, not his usual one, to assess the damage. Couldn't believe the cost. But it was worth it, he thought. It would take a few days for repairs, the dent taken out, the fender repainted. He didn't have time for that. He had plans. He had to pick up Juhan Lipp and begin page two of his adventure. It was his way back to health, he was sure of it.

That night he felt like telling his wife everything. A neat little person, his Emily, with her papers piled carefully beside her, making precise checkmarks with her pencil to define her world. He had always been a loose, sloppy sort of fellow, relaxed some would call it, and he appreciated her tidy exactitude. Like the way she sliced onions crosswise before chopping them into cubes, her thorough rinsing of the lettuce, her snappy manner of breaking ends off string beans before putting them through a little gizmo to sliver them in the French manner. But now she was busy with her papers: filling out forms, making lists, categorizing, consulting statistics, formulating solutions, drawing up personality profiles, analyzing the law of averages, predicting outcomes. Becoming a paper-pusher in spite of herself, trying to find the appropriate slot for each individual, telling students what their aspirations should be according to their personality types, what occupation to pursue, how to behave at the job interview. It was all written down somewhere: what to eat, what to believe, what to accomplish in life, how much money to set aside for retirement, which position worked best for procreation and which was better for a good time, the number of children one should have and how they should be raised, the proper weight, the right amount of exercise, how to clean the teeth or what to soak them in if one hadn't flossed properly during the early years. Assured voices holding out the promise of happiness. All his life Emmanuel had tried to do what was expected of him, burying the small seed of discontent he may always have carried within. It seemed to him now, that something was missing, that something was not right, until it had finally germinated and burst forth on February 4 at 10:42 a.m., and there was nothing he could do about it.

He decided not to interrupt Emily after all. It was not necessary for her to be thoroughly informed about each and every little thing that didn't concern her. Besides, he could predict what she would say. *You're crazy, Emmanuel. You're acting like a teenager. You're trying to escape reality because you're afraid of growing old. You refuse to face facts. You don't know what your function is now that the boys are living their own lives and no one is dependent on you any more. If your work no longer satisfies you, get a hobby. You can look forward to early retirement in ten more years. There must be something in the whole wide world that sparks your interest. Check out the Web. Too bad you're not a reader. There's nothing like a good book to take one's mind off one's own troubles and give one a sense of perspective.*

No, he wouldn't tell her. She approached things from a different viewpoint altogether and the journey he was embarking upon would not fit into her conception of the path his life should follow. And she would never understand why he needed to search so desperately for another woman.

13

"**N**OTHING has a beginning or an end. That is merely a human limitation we place on life. You think by finding this woman, your troubles will be over? Of course you have considered it may bring forth an entirely new set."

The old man was talkative, stimulated by coffee and his cigarette. They had stopped at the same small restaurant for breakfast. Two old boys out on a lark. Juhan lifted his bright blue eyes and gnome face to study the younger man's profile – the down-turned mouth, the deep frown line between the eyebrows – as Emmanuel stopped the car on the shoulder of the highway to set the odometer to zero and write in his pad. FEBRUARY 24, EXIT 15 – EAST DEXTER, he printed in block letters on top of the second page.

"Not that I expect to find anything here," he explained as he pulled back on to the exit ramp. "I'm sure I was farther out in the country than this. But my plan is to conduct the investigation methodically, checking out every exit until I find the right one."

"That is all right with me," said Juhan in his precise English, free of contractions. "I am very glad to be out of the house. This woman you are searching for. What does she look like?"

The image flashing into Emmanuel's consciousness was fuzzy, some parts blocked out, like faces of protected witnesses or the naked breasts of strippers in TV documentaries. To protect the eyes of the innocent. He was sure he would immediately recognize the voice, however – a bit husky, a smoker who had given it up when the children were born – her fingers combing carelessly through dark blond hair, blue jeans tight across her rump. Why was he searching for her, really? He was, admittedly, no longer himself. Could it be possible, then, that he had not actually faced up to true motives? What would have happened had he stayed on her davenport, rather than running off like a frightened rabbit? Juhan was right. His troubles might just be beginning if they did manage to find her.

"Blond. Tall. Good figure. Early thirties, I'd say. A bit rough around the edges. For sure I'd recognize her. And the house. And the little girls. And the dog."

"Does your wife know about this search?" Juhan ventured.

"Well, no," he admitted. "It's not what you think. Besides, I've got you along to protect me." A sideways glance to cement the conspiracy.

But Juhan was not amused.

"Anna, my daughter, married an insufferable fool who could see only his own self and nothing else. She believed in him. In his theories. She did everything to ease his life, thinking it was important to his quest. When he no longer believed in himself, she had nothing left, except her sense of responsibility to her elderly parents. She has never had an opportunity to live a life of her own making."

Emmanuel had stopped listening, letting his imagination wander. Back to her living room. *I knew you were a stranger of course, the moment you arrived,* she was saying. *But I refuse to wither away because John is gone. We don't get many visitors out here in the country, as you can imagine, and I am not the sort to pass up an opportunity when it comes my way. We drew pictures of you. Wanna see?* She brought out three drawings. Smudges of colour from the little girls and her own impression of a red-faced man with an orange moustache in a bright blue Santa suit with the words *THANK YOU MISTER FOR A GOOD TIME* printed underneath. *You should live your life as if you are a permanent part of some-one else's memory,* she said. Or was it Juhan who had said that?

"Myself, I had something quite different in mind also when I first started out," Juhan was explaining. "I intended to be a great statesman. Studied law at university. In the old country. Times were different then. A politician could be a visionary, and also, the other way around."

"What happened?" asked Emmanuel, bringing his attention back to the old man and beginning to view him from an entirely new perspective.

"Well, you know. The War. And the aftermath. I ended up here in this country as a broom pusher. Custodial engineers, we are called these days, I believe. It was a good job. I was damned lucky to get it. We were able to save enough to send Anna to college."

"Your wife?" asked Emmanuel.

"In this country she worked as a charwoman in an office building. When I met her in our youth, she was already an accomplished pianist. Only sixteen, she was invited to play with the Estonian symphony. During all those years we were refugees living in DP camps when she was not able to get near a piano, she said she lost her touch and she would never again play afterwards. 'A concert pianist must practice for hours every day,' she said. 'They have taken my life,' she said. 'I might as well be dead like the rest.' Until the end of her days, my wife was always longing for what was gone forever."

Emmanuel became genuinely interested now. It had been a long while since he had met anyone outside the carpeted world of his own existence, give or take a few individual aberrations. Most men, himself included, could only manage a pale imitation of real despair. Angst. Anxiety. Depression. Dismay. Discontent. Wordily raging at the human condition. But here was someone who experienced what people like himself only read about: a man who truly had lost everything. Only his daughter was left to him. Yet this old fellow was capable of relishing something as simple as a cup of coffee and a cigarette in the company of a foolish stranger.

"How old were you when you left Europe?" Emmanuel asked.

"Thirty-eight," Juhan responded. "Anna was only young. She started in school without knowing a word of English. Graduated high school at the top of her class." He became silent for a time, lost in the past.

"Do you mind if I call you Man?" he finally asked. "Your name seems to wrap itself too tightly around my Estonian tongue."

"Actually my friends call me M," Emmanuel replied a bit sheepishly. "Big M. And my wife is little m. Emily, her name is. We've got two boys, Mike and Gerry. Both away. In college. Gerry's working on a Ph.D. In English." Feeling like a kid telling his story. *Here's my list of credentials, sir, the accomplishments of my life.*

"And what do you do, Man? Do you have a profession? You are too young to be retired, I think, although they do not wait until sixty-five these days. Anna is planning to take her retirement shortly."

"Sick leave," said Emmanuel. "Office job. Paper pusher."

"I see," Juhan said, glancing over at him, but too tactful to pursue it.

They were driving through a conglomeration of the old and new. A few decrepit farmhouses still remaining among those that had been refurbished, some recent constructions mixed in. Suburbia stretching its tentacles.

"Could that be her?" Juhan suddenly cried, pointing at a blond woman in a jogging suit, pushing a baby-carriage and pulling a small dog by a leash.

"No. No," said Emmanuel. "She had a big tan dog. Golden retriever or lab type."

They met with no more possible sightings that day, but agreed to pursue the search again the next morning. Exit 16 might be more promising.

14

WHEN he arrived home, the answering machine was blinking. "Are you there, M?" He heard Emily's voice coming out of the box. "M, are you there?" A click, and then again. "Are you there? Are you all right?" And yet another. "I don't know where you are, but I won't be home till later tonight. I hope everything is all right. We have a meeting." Hesitating, then hanging up.

He'd been found out. She hadn't yet noticed his crumpled fender, but he wouldn't be able to get away with it for long. He'd have to tell her something. *Thought I'd get some fresh air since it was such a nice day,* he would explain. *Drove out to the country. Unfortunately there was a bit of a smash up. Nothing serious. Rear-ended an old fellow.*

"Those old people," said Emily. "Such a hazard on the roadways. They really should do something about it. Mandatory re-licensing tests at seventy. And no one should drive at all when they're eighty years old! It's just not safe."

Who was this woman? Not little m, surely, becoming so certain of her point of view in her later years. Opinionated even, one might call it. Not his sweetheart of yore, a shrinking violet by a mossy stone, half hidden from the eye. In the beginning, he liked to think of her that way, his only concession to Introductory English. Wordsworth, if he remembered correctly. Now, who had become the shrinking violet, taking bumbling refuge under a bristly moustache he no longer possessed, neglecting to reveal to his contentious wife that the old man had his signal light on well before he slowed for the left turn and that it was definitely Emmanuel "M" Taggart, forty-five, daydreaming about a younger woman, still securely protected under the shield of insurance, who was most definitely at fault. To his continuing shame, he persisted in the falsification.

"The old guy had no insurance, so I didn't report it. There's hardly any damage, really. None to his vehicle and just a small dent in my fender. Luckily I wasn't doing the speed limit."

He led her out to the garage to take a look. "I went afterwards to get an estimate. A couple of them, in fact. That's why I wasn't home when you called. Sorry if I worried you."

Lies. Lies. Once you start, it's easy not to stop.

"It's all right, dear," she forgave him, her thoughts already preoccupied, he could tell, with something much more significant: her meetings, her appointments, her preparations for the next day. "I'm glad you're beginning to feel well enough to get out some. Soon you'll be up and at 'em again, you'll see. I picked up some Chinese. Are you hungry?"

With a great sense of relief that the deception was, in part, over, he pretended to enjoy the gristly ribs coated in nail polish, the slimy sprouts, the brown rice concealing its quota of grubs and maggots and rat shit.

"Yum, yum," he lied. "Haven't had Chinese for ages."

She gazed at him with her eyes brimming. "Maybe you are getting better, M. Truly. 'Winter is the time when everything rests – when the Earth withdraws its energy.'" He could tell she was quoting someone, one of her "sources," from the way her voice changed to a lower, more sonorous pitch.

When she came over to collect his garbage – the plastic utensils and Styrofoam box containing the remains of his supper – he pulled her over to sit on his lap.

"You seem different without your moustache," she said, nuzzling his neck.

She seemed different also. Didn't smell quite the same. Spent her time in places foreign to him. Meeting with people who thought they knew things. Taking notes.

"What is happening to us?" he mumbled.

"Hush," she said. "Spring is on the way."

But the news that night predicted snow. Freezing rain after midnight with a heavy snowfall warning for the whole region.

"Yippee!" shouted Emily like a little kid and set the alarm for 6:15 so she could listen for the school closing announcements.

At 6:25 she shouted, "Yippee!" again and snuggled in close. "The roads are impassable," she whispered huskily, sliding her hand down his body, rubbing gently between his legs.

Emmanuel was not able to rise to the occasion. He remained in hibernation and soon she sighed and rolled over, plumping her pillow and sinking her head into another few hours of sweet, lazy, early morning sleep.

15

NOT yet fully awake, he could smell Sunday morning when they were still a family. Before the boys grew up. Before Emily turned her energies outward. Eating together at the table at ten or eleven, something special: brunch. A second cup of coffee carried into the sunny living room for a leisurely perusal of the Sunday papers. M and m, taking a well-deserved break from their familial duties. Relaxing. Companionable. Sharing the joke, the item of interest, commenting on the most recent foibles of mankind. Together working out the *Times* crossword puzzle. Watching the game with the boys in the family room later, while Emily prepared dinner. The Day of Rest.

Dawdling half-asleep under the covers, dreaming sweet morning dreams, blissfully relieved at last of the frightful nightmares engendered in the darkness of night, his arms wrapped around the downy pillow, Emmanuel yearned to remain forever in the warm peaceful glow of those bygone days which, at the time, he had taken totally for granted and accepted without question as his due.

"Emmanuel," Emily called. "Breakfast is ready. Time to rise and shine!"

What did she have to chirp about? No one could

escape the inevitable. He could not bear the thought of rising, of putting on his robe and slippers, of brushing his teeth. Pulled the covers over his head instead.

But she would not let him be.

She had set the table in the dining room and carried in an enormous platter of scrambled eggs, garnered with crisp strips of bacon, surrounded by home fries. A basket of warm blueberry muffins. A large slab of butter. Freshly squeezed orange juice. Hot coffee. Silently they consumed, the Lord and Lady of the Manor, at opposite ends of the long table, gazing out into a world transformed by snow, large flakes still falling.

The last time they had eaten here was Christmas, preferring now to take their meals in front of the TV. Mike had made it home for a few days, but Gerry spent the holidays with his girlfriend's family out west. Nothing was like it used to be. It was almost a strain to pretend to be jolly by eating and drinking too much. On Boxing Day, they usually made the long trek to Emily's parents', but the roads being treacherous, the trip was cancelled. Mike went skiing with his friends instead.

"You're a marvel, Em," Emmanuel groaned, pushing apart the scraps remaining on his plate so it didn't look like he left too much. Definitely his stomach had shrunk. Out of long-time habit, she had prepared enough food for a whole family. To be scraped now into Tupperware containers, only to be rediscovered weeks later in the back recesses of the refrigerator, transformed into something else entirely.

Feeling guilty, he helped her clear the table. Companionably they loaded the dishwasher, as Emily chattered on about the boys, about Gerry's girlfriend – *They shared an apartment, but was it really serious?* – about Mike's plans to head south for March Break – *You're only young once, after all, and he did promise to stop in and visit Gran.* They were lucky, considering all the pitfalls of this modern age, that the kids had both turned out just fine.

His boys, Emmanuel thought, his heart turning mushy with love and softening his face. Gerry, the thinker. Furrows already developing between the young brows. *But Dad, this is serious. We can do something. It's still possible. If only we all got together on it.* Power to the people. His shoulders hunched, bearing the weight. Writing term papers. Preparing for Orals. Researching his dissertation. And Mike, the opposite. Sunny. Life his lark. Enjoy it while you can. Grinning hugely, slapping the old man on the shoulder. *How's it hangin, Dad?* Emmanuel smiled within.

"What are you looking so smug about?" Emily asked.

"They're good boys," he said. "All things considered."

"I do miss them," she said. "Though I'm glad they're gone."

Gone, gone. Gone like John. He couldn't get the phrase out of his mind as Emily jabbered happily about how nice it was to shop just for two, how much easier to keep the house clean, how rewarding she found her job. Finally she was doing what she herself wanted to do. And more of the same. Half of it he couldn't hear because she had her back to him, putting away the accouterments of their feast. An advertisement for the Empty Nest: *Rejuvenated Mum Finds New Life.*

The father, having lost his role, spends his days seeking a younger woman out in the country somewhere off Exit 16 or 17. He had stopped listening and let his mind wander back to a simpler world where the breadwinner returns from the office to the smells of Italian cooking, the enthusiastic wag of the dog, two dimpling little girls, and a large glass of foamy home-brew brought to him by a welcoming woman in tight jeans, a bit rough around the edges.

"You're smiling again," remarked Emily. "Nothing like a big breakfast to bring the roses to a man's cheeks." Playfully she patted him on the rear. "Feeling better?" she asked.

"Still shimmery around the eyes and wobbly in the legs," he answered, taking his bulk to the comfort of the sofa. "Little Miss Dr. Whatshername might not find anything wrong with me, but that doesn't mean I'm A-OK. There are all sorts of syndromes floating about. Just listen to the news. They're discovering new ones daily. And I'm NOT going back to work until I'm good and ready." Emmanuel getting himself riled up now. "It isn't as though my lowly job is essential to human survival, and God knows I've built up enough sick leave to stay out for several years. They should hand out medals at the office like they did in elementary school for perfect attendance. Always there, ready and willing, in his little cubicle, Mr. Taggart. You can depend on him."

"You don't need to justify yourself to me, dear. I believe you."

Condescendingly supportive, his devoted wife.

"Oh? Has someone been saying something behind my back?" he responded, bristling. "That I'm a shirker? That this is all pretence?" Anger rising up. Roses in the cheeks getting redder. Coffee cup on the table next to him in fear of flying.

"Tut. Tut," she calmed him. "No one has said any-thing. As a matter of fact, everyone is quite concerned.

People just don't know what's proper to say in a case like this. They act super-jovial, talk about normal things: the weather, sports scores, the latest political scandal. They don't want to face the silence, the inevitable question that remains in back of their minds."

"What question is that?" he asked curtly, still angry.

"How long?"

How long? How LONG? They were all expecting him to die? This thought took him aback a pace, his anger dissipating like a fart in the wind, as his father-in-law, old Abelard, was fond of saying. He had been willing to settle upon a gradual decline, maybe even a slightly debilitating condition, something rare but curable, if not now, then certainly soon, with all the latest medical breakthroughs they were coming up with. But she seemed to be insisting that he face facts. The beginning and the end. Juhan said the concept was indicative of human limitation. A man begins to die when he is born. Is he dead before the moment of conception as well? Only his death is certain. The chances of his actually being born are quite extraordinary.

He turned on the TV to relieve his mind. Flipped the remote until he found an action movie. Tires squealing. Cars exploding. Heroes killing bad guys. Man stuff. He was sick and tired of the blathering of women. Getting used to being by himself in the house. Belching at will. Using the bathroom with the door open. Staring into the mirror at his ragged self. Lying on the sofa in his striped robe, his flaccid manhood exposed, cooling off.

16

BUT Emily wouldn't leave him be.

"Hope the roads will be better by tomorrow night when the Smithers come," she remarked brightly, gazing out of the window at the snow-covered yard.

"What?" he hollered, but softly, not in his usual form, half of his attention still preoccupied by gunplay, blood splattering inside the TV screen. "WHAT!"

"I told you days ago. I invited them for dinner. Don't you remember? Now, M, don't get all hot under the collar. It will do you a world of good. You've been cooped up here for a couple of months without seeing a soul. Except for those in the medical profession, of course."

She better not smile, not even the slightest twitch in the corner of her lip or the coffee cup would fly. He already had it by the handle, but she managed to keep her composure.

"Seriously, M. You've got to see people. To take your mind off yourself. It'll cheer you up, you'll see. It does you no good to brood here alone day after day imagining God knows what. Honestly. I bought some Chianti. I'll cook lasagne. We'll make an occasion of it. Candlelight and wine!"

A pregnant pause.

Then another volley in a different tone. Her enthusiasm deflated. His patient long-suffering spouse in sickness and in health, till death do us part, resorting to a servile whine. "If you want me to, I'll call them up and cancel. Tell them you're not fit for company."

"Don't bother," he huffed, not acknowledging her sarcasm, pretending to turn his attention back to the movie. "I'll try my best to be civil to these people – even though 'I'm not myself,' as you have pointed out to the world on numerous occasions – but only because it seems to be so important to you."

It was a game they had played for several weeks now. Passing the guilt back and forth like a tennis ball, looking for the best shot, backing the opponent into a corner, then angling the missile hard across the net to the other side, winning the point, the outcome of the set still in question.

"You remember the Smithers? You met them last summer at the Faculty Picnic. You said they were nice."

Faintly he recalled playing horseshoes with a hardy bald man in a blue golf shirt rounded over tan Bermuda shorts which revealed vulnerable heavily veined white legs seldom exposed to the elements. A wife who squealed like a frightened piglet, jumping up and down and clapping her hands whenever he scored a point. Ted and Lily?

"Ted and Lila," she corrected his thoughts. "He's in insurance or something."

"I'm sure it will be a lovely evening," he said with just enough ambivalence so she could take it as she wanted.

"That's the spirit," she said, carrying his coffee cup to the kitchen. Not in a mood for a real battle, his wife. Giving up. Forfeiting the point. "They're the ones I told you about who are into alternative medicine," she called back to him over her shoulder. "I'm sure they'll be happy to share with you. Give you some pointers."

So that was the real reason for this dinner party. A slam in the corner by the little m. Not giving up at all. Removed his coffee cup as a preventive measure before the volley, knowing him to be a sore loser. He heard her in the kitchen clanking dishes, humming to herself. And what did he have to look forward to? The Smithers and their stupid propaganda. Happily giving him pointers. Thinking they had the world by the balls.

Disgusted with his life and everyone in it, he beat the pillow viciously before settling down his bristly head, turning his face to the blue-flecked upholstery, feigning sleep. But his brain was riled up, his belly stuffed with grease and rumbling, his soul hollow. *We are the hollow men, we are the stuffed men...* another remembrance from English Lit 101. Perhaps Gerry wasn't pursuing such an inferior profession after all. A middle man. An English professor. Pontificating upon the learned thoughts of others. Offering a watered-down version to throngs of lacklustre students to make them feel good about themselves. *Look, Ma! Look what I found! A novel idea! An epigram! A striking metaphor! An epiphany!*

Hollow. Hollow. He felt as hollow as a hot air balloon. A man of no moral stance, of no political persuasion, of no religious preference, of no fixed ideas. The major issues that others spoke so passionately about left him cold. Capital punishment, abortion, prayer in the schools, crime in the streets. Generalizations bothered him. Slogans merely, formulated to garner mass appeal. Yet he was full of definite opinions. Emily could attest to that. Working himself into a purple rage over specific instances of injustice or pain, weeping silently in his heart. Now his balloon had popped, the gas rumbling uncomfortably in his gut as it fizzed out of him.

Despite all his grumbling, by Saturday evening he had resigned himself to the idea of company and was even beginning to get into the spirit of the preparations, showering and shaving, stepping on the scale to note he was almost ten pounds lighter, trimly pulling up his belt a notch, turning sideways to appreciate his new profile in the bedroom mirror. Getting back to his fighting weight. It was true what they said: losing a few pounds did make a person appear younger – in candlelight, if you didn't look too closely.

Emily prided herself on being the perfect hostess and had spent the day getting ready, part of the presentation now covered with plastic wrap in the refrigerator, the remainder keeping warm in the oven, filling the air with the garlicky aroma of her special sauce, the dining room festive with their wedding china and silver, handing him a chilled glass rimmed with salt. "Cheers," she said, "Handsome." Quite fetching herself in slimming black, her cheeks pink, eyes darkened by makeup.

The whole evening, actually, went much better than he expected, he reflected later, all things considered, although the little m might be harbouring a small grudge. By the time the Smithers arrived, Emmanuel had felt quite light-headed from the stiff drink in his empty stomach.

"You remember Ted and Lila?" Emily doing the honours. "My husband M?"

"Nice to see you again, M," said Ted smoothly, reaching out a hand, exuding his successful businessman's assurance like expensive cologne.

He was not the chubby one tossing horseshoes that

Emmanuel remembered. Ted Smithers was a tall man with thick curly dark hair greying at the temples, who worked out at the gym regularly, judging by the abs that definitely rippled under his silk shirt as he removed his distressed leather jacket. His wife Lila, however, a small sprightly redhead, chirpy and perky, he definitely could recall jumping up and down in shorts and halter, squealing like a pig.

Happily, the wintry weather and the condition of the roads provided sufficient preliminary conversation to get them comfortably through the *hors d'œuvres* and into the dining room. Then the business of eating, the compliments to the chef. It wasn't until after dessert, when they took their second cup of coffee into the living room that the main topic of the evening was finally broached.

"So I hear you haven't been feeling well lately," Ted remarked soberly, by way of introduction. Three pairs of eyes stared intently at Emmanuel, waiting for his response so the flow of words could begin and the message proclaimed, the truth revealed, the advice proffered, so the *raison d'etre* for the evening's festivities could finally be laid out on the table.

There was a long gaping pause as Emmanuel carefully set down his coffee cup, leaned back against the cushions of the couch and looked intently at each of his interrogators in turn. He was prepared for this. But his teeth were zippered shut and he said nothing. The four of them sat in silence, discomfiture building up like steam in a pressure cooker, until Emily, as the responsible hostess, finally released the valve and deflated the evening.

"It's just a flu or something, we figure, that's been hanging on," she excused him. "We're coping."

The Smithers, Ted and Lila, left shortly after, their mission aborted. When the door closed Emily pinched her lips and encompassed his entire person in a glare of intense loathing.

"What?" he said, smugly innocent. "Did I say something wrong?"

She didn't answer, just walked away from him with her load and started clearing up. Match point! He had won the set.

17

THEY spent the following day quietly, each pretending the other did not exist, a common enough condition for the In-Betweeners – elderly Empty Nesters who have not yet experienced the onset of grandchildren which restores the comforting balance of family obligations. Ostentatiously preoccupied – Emmanuel watching basketball on TV; Emily doing homework, collating all children into four basic personality types – both of them fretfully picking at leftover lasagne, anxious for the weekend to be over so they could get away from one another entirely to resume their personal pursuits.

Emmanuel now had a viable excuse to be out of the house in case his absence was detected, for it was imperative to get the car repaired, although Emily didn't seem to care where he spent his time and seemed in no mood to check up on him for several days at least. Monday morning he would call Juhan to confirm their arrangement to do Exit 16 together. Away from the prying eyes and judgemental evaluations of women. Free at last! He was looking forward to spending more time with the old man, enjoying the sound of the rollicking R's in his speech. It was as pleasant to listen to him talk as to watch someone with a good appetite devour a delicious meal. Juhan certainly knew what life was all about, yet there was something childlike about him. An honesty, Emmanuel decided, his responses fresh and immediate, free of artifice or calculation, or the boredom of habit. *We cannot see unless we look. We cannot hear unless we listen. We cannot feel unless we hurt. We cannot love unless we feel.* Who said that? Like airy particles of debris, the words floated aimlessly in the oceans of his mind.

But when he telephoned the next morning, there was a woman's voice on the answering machine. Anna, the daughter, he presumed. He left no message, tried again later with the same result. It was certainly possible that Juhan had forgotten all about their clandestine meeting, or that something else had come up. The old man had mentioned spells. Apprehensive, he drove out, nevertheless.

No one came when he rang the buzzer. Furtively, he turned the knob on the front door, but it was locked. Should he peer in the windows? A stranger in a blue great-coat. Too suspicious, in case there happened to be a neighbourhood watch. Explaining to the constable: *There's a sick old man in there, Officer. Could you break down the door?*

In actual fact, he had made no definite plans with Juhan. Nor had he left his number. Just expected him to be there the next day. *See you tomorrow*, he had said. But Friday the roads were impassable and then the weekend intervened. He walked around the perimeter of the house, exaggerating his motions, making them larger than life so there would be no mistaken impression that he was sneaking around, up to no good, if someone was indeed watching. Should he inquire of the neighbours? Ask if anyone knew the whereabouts of Juhan Lipp? That seemed a bit extreme, even to Emmanuel. After all, they hardly knew each other. It was more than likely that the old man had an appointment somewhere.

With a deep sense of dismay and foreboding nevertheless, he drove to the restaurant where they had coffee the week before with a ridiculous faint hope of finding Juhan there, but there were no cars parked in front and the place looked empty. He had no intention of pursuing his quest without the old man. This was something they were going to do together. They shook hands on it.

There seemed to be no recourse but to drive back home, keep trying the number. Pacing the floor. Working himself into a state of worry he hadn't felt since the boys were in their teens, late with the car. What message could he leave? He didn't want to get the old man in trouble. The daughter might not take kindly to her sickly father gallivanting around with a stranger, drinking coffee and smoking cigarettes, searching the countryside for a blond in tight jeans.

When the phone rang that night, Emily answered.

"Some woman for you," she said, looking him full in the face, her eyes narrowed, hovering nearby so she could hear every word he was saying.

"You don't know me," said the voice familiar to him already, he had heard it so many times on the answering machine each time he had called Juhan's number. "My father, Juhan Lipp, asked that I telephone you. It seems you had some sort of an appointment?"

"Yes?" he said, noncommittal.

"My father's in hospital," the voice continued. "At the Queens. He had a slight stroke Friday night."

"Sorry to hear that," Emmanuel said. "Thanks so

much for letting me know."

Emily still hovering, her eyebrows raised.

"It's the old man," he explained. "From the accident. That was his daughter. He's in hospital."

"O, NO!" Her mouth forming the words even before the vocal cords had their say.

"O, no," he echoed, "not because of the accident. At least I don't think so."

"Why did she call *you* then?" Emily asked, not letting him get away with any vague dissimulations. He had to be careful not to say too much, just enough to satisfy her.

"He's had a stroke. He's confused."

Emily had assumed her interrogative pose, both hands on her hips, invading his personal space. He must think fast now.

"He remembers having a car accident. Thinks he may have killed the other driver, apparently. Heh, heh. I should probably go visit him. Show him I'm still alive and kicking, though barely. Heh, heh. Set him straight." He could see she didn't believe him.

"How did she get your number?" she demanded, staring straight into his evasive eyes, measuring the length and breadth of his confabulation.

"I gave him my business card. Most likely. When we had the collision. I'll just go to the Queens tomorrow and check what's up with the old fellow. Straighten him out. Don't worry, Emily, for godsakes. It's not high drama." On the attack now. Employing diversionary tactics. "You always do like to make such a big deal out of every little misfortune. Worry will make you old before your time," he teased to soften her up.

"Okay, M," she allowed, backing off, but not

through with him yet. "Maybe in your present condition you shouldn't be driving either."

"My capabilities aren't diminished, my dear, only my energy," he replied curtly, slouching off, retreating to the couch to turn on the TV and stare at the screen, to collect his thoughts and examine his words to see if he needed to patch up his story before the loopholes became too obvious.

Why couldn't he just have told her the truth? he asked himself later. He wasn't, after all, conducting a torrid and adulterous affair, or even a casual flirtation. He was merely trying to right a wrong in the company of an aged and respectable friend. Why should she be so suspicious anyway, listening in on his conversations, watching him like a hawk, trying to entrap him with her clever questioning? Now it was his turn to stare with suspicious narrowed eyes at the back of her head, fortunately, or he would have to explain himself once again.

All their married life, he had been a faithful husband. Few men could claim that out loud, judging by what he'd heard, both statistically and as lascivious gossip around the office. Not that there hadn't been some opportunities, a couple of temptations, and, if he were to be perfectly honest, one or two instances of communal drunkenness where it wasn't his fault that things didn't develop further than the preliminaries. Still, he had done nothing much to be ashamed of, being a healthy red-blooded North American male.

A man thinks of sex every ten seconds. He had heard that somewhere. An exaggeration, to be sure. It depended on age. *I wouldn't mind having her shoes under my bed,* his father used to joke as some under-clad ripening nymphet displayed herself on TV. He had forced a smile, but found the old man's leering countenance lingering in his memory like an unpleasant aftertaste and was always careful around his own sons never to reveal the presence of random lust. Unlike most other men of his acquaintance. Fathers watching their boys on the basketball court, making lewd comments about the tight little buttocks of cheerleaders, girls young enough to be their daughters. He was a breast man himself.

Emily, though, had always been slightly jealous, he thought. Suspicious without due cause. Questioning. Inspecting his person with a proprietary air, sucking in her lower lip. *Just looking, dear*, he would tease. He never had any doubts about her and he told her so numerous times. He made no objections when she was upgrading her degree and would spend nights in the city because the roads were bad. It never even entered his mind to check up on her. But then, women were different. Didn't have the same urges, despite what the feminist literature proclaimed nowadays.

18

EMMANUEL hated hospitals.

It was her fault, Emily's, that he was forced into this predicament. If she hadn't questioned him, he wouldn't have lied. Now he was committed to this visit "to straighten the old man out."

Trudging through the thick germ-laden air of the long corridor, his shoes creaking on polished vinyl, trying not to stare at the sick and dying as he passed the open doorways, squeezed into the back corner of the elevator by a large cart bearing a mummified individual with open mouth and frightened eyes. *Excuse me. Excuse me. I need to get out here. I need some fresh air, a field of green grass, a mountain stream, a ray of sunshine, twittering songbirds, the beauty of creation. I DON'T BELONG HERE.* Gawping into the stuffy rooms to find Juhan Lipp in number 32, seeing instead a man with his arms strapped to the sides of his bed, calling, "Mona, Mona," and beyond him on the far side by the window, a withered crone with sunken cheeks under a cloud of white hair.

"John?" he inquired.

The head turned slightly and Emmanuel recognized the blue eyes.

"It's Emmanuel. Emmanuel Taggart? Man?" he said, feeling foolish. Obviously the old fellow had no re-collection of their brief acquaintance, for he abruptly swivelled his head away toward the window and fumbled for something in the drawer of the small cabinet beside his bed. When he turned back, he looked more like himself.

"My teeth," he said. "I always give them a rest when I sleep. I was not expecting company. It is nice to see you, Man. Sit down. Sit down. Anna must have called you?"

"She told me you were in hospital, yes," Emmanuel said. "Thought I'd come and see for myself."

"I am just taking a small vacation at the finest hotel in the world. They provide you with everything here. Three square meals a day. Sponge baths. Backrubs. Bedpans. They even wipe your ass for you if you are willing to wait a few hours. As long as you still have your wits about you, that is. The poor old gentleman over there" – he motioned with his eyes – "is not so lucky. He has been calling for Mona ever since I got here, but she has not yet arrived. They have to tie him down or he would go searching for her. Starving to death, I figure. A volunteer came to feed him once, but the nurses, they are too busy most of the time."

Emmanuel could think of no response. Pressed his lips together and nodded solemnly several times like a man with palsy. It was up to the patient to entertain his visitor.

"So did you find her yet?"

"What?" In these surroundings he had forgotten all about his foolish obsession.

"The woman you are searching for?" Juhan elaborated.

"No. No. I figure that's something we must accomplish together. When are they letting you out of here?" Emmanuel asked.

"They are testing me. Poking and prying here and there. Photographing my insides. Analyzing my circuits. Trying to find the cause for the present difficulty. I am an old man. They have not found a cure for that yet. I have heard they are about to clone beloved pets, however. With human beings such procedures may be more complicated. Genes only remember the DNA, not a lifetime of memories. You could end up with a different person altogether. The same old argument persists: free will versus predetermination. Now, what did you ask me?"

In fine form, old Juhan. Under the white sheet his body looked shrunken, but his mind remained as vigorous as ever, roaming through past and present, admiring the view.

"Any man who believes he has figured out Creation, has died before his time. Our brains are happiest discovering. Once we sum up, it's all over."

His eyes alive with process. No stodgy prefabricated ancient sentiments here. Time-honoured ideas maybe, but constantly revised when new material became available.

Emmanuel promised to come again. The next day. Not from any sense of obligation this time, but because he wanted to. With Juhan he felt a respite from the despair that had so suddenly enveloped him. The old man possessed *joie de vivre* even in his present circumstances. Maybe the fellow in the next bed had found it also. Perhaps he was calling for Mona not from the depths of his pain but in appreciation of a memory. It was hard to tell for sure, but pleasant to think so.

19

EXPLAINING to Emily. Fashioning the truth to fit the image he wished to project for himself: The Good Samaritan, Big M, holding out a helping hand, giving succour to the infirm, cheering up the lonely, despite his own physical decline and his nearly pathological abhorrence of hospitals. Patting himself firmly on the back, SINCE NOBODY ELSE WILL. Pointing that fact out to his sharp-eyed little wife.

"What about the daughter?" asked Emily. "Why isn't she around to comfort him?"

"She's working. A mathematician." He emphasized the word as if revealing some kind of rare disease. "About ready to retire, he says."

"What's she look like?" Not appeased yet, his loving spouse.

"Haven't seen head nor tail of her," he said, quite inappropriately to the circumstances. Appeasing, cajoling, telling half-truths, little white lies. Why? He hadn't done anything wrong. He was behaving like an imbecile, treating his partner-for-life like a two-year-old child. Couldn't either of them handle reality?

"Truth? Truth is a slippery wench," said Juhan. "It depends on the moment. And women, practiced as they are in the art of deceit themselves, can smell out the slightest falsehood even if they cannot quite sniff out the whole story. Anna, my daughter, she could tell right away something was not right. Her nose in the air picking up scents here and there, she kept after me until I had to, finally, tell her everything."

Emmanuel was discomfited, not sure whether his character could withstand the telling of his foolish tale.

"Oh, not your story," said Juhan quickly. "Only my own small part in it. About the accident, about smoking cigarettes and drinking coffee, confessing my sins. Made up something about insurance and asked her to call you to cancel our appointment. She was angry. Threatened me with a babysitter. I told her, one has to prize the moment. That is not a libertine statement. It does not necessarily give license to indulge in what is forbidden. It simply means one should always fully apprehend one's life. Like an infant, if you will. Fascinated by every aspect of the world around it.

"But I am talking too much," he said, leaning back against the pillows. "Must be the steroids they are pumping into me to build up my strength. Not doing much for decrepitude, but definitely activating the old brain. It is a windy day in there. Brainwaves crashing onto the rocky shore one after another. Very refreshing. It makes my face red and my tongue work overtime."

Indeed, he did look like a small bright-cheeked elf, Santa's helper from the Old World, with his shock of white hair awry and his blue eyes sparkling.

"Lying here I am youthful again, contemplating man's role in the Universe as we did in my student days in Estonia. With this important difference: Now I look upon such philosophical meanderings as pure nonsense, an intellectual word game merely; then I took myself much more seriously, anticipating that my individual presence on this planet would truly make a difference. It is interesting to consider, don't you think, the consciousness of man. The errant creature in all Creation. Out of the 1.5 million terrestrial species that have been described and classified by scientists, and the 5 to 50 million that have not yet been discovered – I recall reading those statistics somewhere – the only one aware of its own existence, able to consciously perceive and change its environment, is a human. Why? It is as if the Creator, done with evolving a world, required someone to apprehend the complexities of the Creation. Like a writer needs a reader, a musician a listener, an artist a viewer with eyes to see. Someone to stand in awe and wonder. Someone to discover and appreciate. But true admiration can only come through imitation. It is only when you try to do something yourself that you fully begin to appreciate a master's touch. Unfortunately, human beings have generally regarded their own species as superior to all else and have used their creative intelligence and opposing thumb not to imitate but to destroy and to aspire to become Masters of the Universe themselves."

Juhan stopped to take a sip of water.

"A failed experiment is mankind. A species doomed by its own arrogance to be the cause of its own extinction."

By the following afternoon the storm had stilled. When Emmanuel arrived, Juhan was asleep, his body making hardly a mound in the rumpled bedding, his face pale now, his toothless mouth agape, his bright eyes closed. The bed next to him was empty, covered over by a clean white sheet.

"John?" Emmanuel whispered, but the old man did not stir. For some time he sat quietly by the bed until a loudspeaker announced that visiting hours were over. Crowding into the elevator then with others still healthy enough to leave this sterile confinement where, under the auspices of uniformed specialists, the two most momentous events of human life were taking place: birth and death. To take a breath of fresh cold air. To brush newly fallen snow off the car. To regard the delicate patterns drawn by tree branches against the heavy clouds. To apprehend the streak of sunlight emerging in the western sky. To stand in awe and wonder at the beauty and terror of the Universe.

20

CAREFULLY he drove down the highway towards home, opening the door of the empty house, agitating the creatures that lodged there, not the amorphous spirits he had himself formerly created, but a few of the 1.5 million real ones, and maybe some that were not yet classified and described: spiders trapping prey inside their intricate webs; fruit flies magically appearing to feed off rotting bananas in the bowl on the counter; speedy silverfish hiding in the cupboard under the sink; minute aphids chewing the leaves of Emily's prized begonia; millions of germs everywhere living out their invisible lives; his own body teeming with purposeful activity, a complex ecosystem doing its thankless job of keeping him alive and moving; the magnificent array of unperceived creation right here in his own living room.

And the red eye of the answering machine blinking, blinking in the silence. He couldn't bring himself to press the message button. *No news is good news*, his mother used to say. As long as he was ignorant of the facts, he could keep the old man safely alive in his mind.

When Emily got home, the light was still flashing.

"There's a message here, M. How come you didn't check it?"

"Didn't notice."

A female voice he vaguely recognized, but not Anna's. Dr. Malick's receptionist. Due to a cancellation, the specialist, Dr. Acton, would see him next Friday at 10 a.m. at the Dawson Clinic.

"The patient must have died while waiting to be diagnosed," Emmanuel sniffed.

"Well, that's good," decided Emily. "You might find out something. How are you feeling these days, anyway? I haven't heard you complain so much lately."

Strained relations still since the visit of Ted and Lila. Both partners preoccupied with their own separate lives. Not sharing their intimate secrets, if any. Emmanuel took out a fly swatter, waited until the multi-faceted eye stopped its watchful gaze and the insect busied itself once again to search the table for crumbs, then let him have it. So much then for awe. He too could be Master of his Universe.

The next day, however, despite Emmanuel's fears of the night before, Juhan was awake and chipper when he got there, the other bed now occupied by a man with a tube up his nose and chemical soup dripping into his veins.

"They are about finished with me here," Juhan said. "I will be dispatched within a few days. Missed you yesterday."

"I was here," said Emmanuel, "but you were sleeping. I didn't want to wake you."

"They took me off steroids. After all that turbulence, I guess they thought I needed a rest. Anna also got an earful. Enough for both ears, actually. They cannot keep an old politician down. Even when the body gives out, the mouth keeps yammering. But all those fine sentiments end up being just words. And words are not capable of sustaining a life. A spoonful of mush offered by a kindly volunteer is much more significant."

"Your old neighbour?" Emmanuel whispered, indicating toward the new patient.

"Gone. It must have happened while I was sleeping. When I woke up they had the bed made up ready for the next customer."

The following afternoon the bed Juhan had occupied was also empty, the new patient in the other bed still comatose, kept alive by the advancements of modern medicine. Emmanuel inquired at the desk.

"Juhan Lipp is no longer with us," the nurse replied, shuffling through a packet of pink forms.

"Has he gone home then?"

"Are you a relative?"

"Just a friend."

"I'm sorry, I cannot give out that information."

Immediately he called. From the lobby of the hospital. The daughter's voice on the answering machine. He tried again when he got home. Same old message. Pacing the floor. Chewing the skin on the side of his forefinger. An urgent demand in his bowels. Something must be wrong. But then again, Juhan had said he would soon be leaving, and the nurse may have merely followed bureaucratic procedure. He knew the ins and outs of that, being in the paper shuffling business himself. It worked well to obfuscate, to protect the incompetent, to spread out responsibility so thinly no one could be called to account. He should have lied. Said he was a long lost son. They were probably on their way home right now. He called again. Or perhaps she was busy settling him in, didn't want to bother answering the phone.

"What's wrong with you, M?" Emily asked. "You seem so agitated tonight. Are you worried about this appointment with the specialist? It's better to know, M, no matter what the verdict," she reassured him.

"Yes. No," replied Emmanuel. He wished he could try calling again, but he was in no mood to explain to Emily and get her all worked up. Tomorrow he would drive out to the house and see what was what.

21

A tall woman with a cloud of white wavy hair and Juhan's blue eyes opened the door.

"Yes?" she said.

"Miss Lipp?" Emmanuel inquired. "Emmanuel Taggart here," he introduced himself, extending his hand.

He could see that she took the hand he proffered with some reluctance, looking with surprised disdain at this man she didn't know, who was shuffling about uncomfortably on her front doorstep, clad in a bright-blue, down-filled greatcoat.

"Anna Fedora," she corrected him. "What can I do for you, Mr. Taggart?"

"Your father—"

"Dead," she interrupted brusquely. "Died two days ago in hospital. Massive heart attack. You've come, I presume, about the insurance?"

"What?" Emmanuel said, taken aback until he remembered Juhan's confabulations. No wonder she looked upon him with such distaste, recalling that she was forced to call him to cancel some sort of an appointment, and then, seeing his name on the answering machine, she must have assumed he was calling to hound her about the insurance.

"No, no, no, no," he defended himself. "I'm a friend of your father's. I mean I came to see him. I didn't realize...no one told me...I'm very sorry, Miss Lipp, Anna, Mrs. Fedora, to hear that he...Please forgive me." He put his hand to his forehead and then brought it down over his eyes, squeezing the bridge of his nose. But she continued to look at him with her level gaze, not saying anything to help him out.

After a moment, he spoke again: "I don't know how much your father told you about me, but what started out as an unfortunate accident became something else entirely. I feel, felt, very close to your father. I've been to visit him every day he's been in hospital. Yesterday they told me he was no longer there. I was hoping he was better, that they sent him home. I called here but got your answering machine. I thought I'd come and see for myself. And the accident was my fault. Totally. I wasn't paying attention to the road."

Anna Fedora still regarded him coldly, obviously waiting for him to take his leave so she could close the door.

But Emmanuel was too riled up now to stop. He had to defend himself. He had to right a wrong and he could only do that by babbling nonsense.

"Your father told me a lot about you, but to tell the truth, I envisioned you quite differently," he said. "What I expected was a grey-haired, tight-lipped hag in bifocals, wearing a cardigan and sensible shoes. A math teacher about to retire. And here *you* are!" He smiled at her then, at Juhan Lipp's beautiful daughter. How could she not invite him in?

She led him through to the back of the house into the kitchen, bright with morning sunlight. Straight lines.

Right angles. Functional furniture free of ornamentation. Everything neat and in its place. It was quite obvious that Anna Fedora appreciated order and disdained excess. Large windows overlooked the backyard, clumps of birch trees shining against the darkness of a dense growth of forest, unexpected privacy in the midst of suburban togetherness. The kitchen was furnished sparingly, everything white except the stainless steel appliances and the large oak table by the window. Anna brought coffee in dark blue ceramic mugs.

"It's wonderful," he remarked, "this room. So spare, so precise, so uncluttered, such a private view."

"I teach mathematics," she said. "I like things to be orderly. I appreciate discipline and control, and problems that have solutions. Cream? Sugar? One or two?" she asked, lifting the white cubes with delicate silver tongs. "Mr. Taggart?"

"You look so young," he blurted out. "What I mean is," he stammered, "to have such an old father."

"He waited until the war was over to have a child," she said. "Sugar?"

"Thank you," Emmanuel said, reaching for the mug and taking a large gulp, relieved to have a prop as a diversion from his blundering, hoping that the caffeine would clear his head.

"You were born in Estonia also?" he asked.

"No. In Austria actually. We were refugees there."

"So how old were you when you came here?"

"Just a child."

He took another sip from his mug, aware that he was acting boorish. This woman had lost her father. There were appropriate things one should say, but he could think of nothing.

"I'm so sorry for your loss," he finally mumbled, clearing his throat, the hackneyed words lying raw and clumsy on the polished surface of the table between them.

"Unfortunately death is the price we pay for being alive," she replied, brushing back her white hair with slim fingers unadorned by rings, the perfect ovals of her nails shining silver in the sunlight. Cool. Controlled. A mathematician. Aware of the undeniable formulas which support all existence.

"My father was eighty-six years old," she continued. "His greatest wish was to die before he lost his mental faculties. 'If I die suddenly,' he told me, 'you must not grieve.' So I am not unhappy. I miss his presence but I have prepared myself for his absence. He was cremated immediately. He didn't want a funeral or a memorial service of any kind. 'Who is there to remember me?' he said, 'and what would they remember? An old fool in his dotage. Those who saw me in my prime are all dead.' Also, I think he wanted to save me the trouble and the expense and the emotional strain. He was very considerate in his own way."

Quickly she took their empty cups to the sink, turning her back to him.

"Will you be having family over or something, so you won't be here all alone?" he dared to ask.

"There is no family. I have no children. I've spent much time alone for many years now," she said. "I don't mind."

But Emmanuel needed something more. To walk out of this house was to walk out of Juhan's life forever. He had grown to love that old man. He needed words spoken in memory. He wanted a closure more elaborate than this. When his own father died there was a big hoopla: relatives gathered at the family homestead, Amanda and her crew, Emily and himself and the boys, various aunts and uncles and cousins. Lots of food, he remembered, casseroles and sweets. A blur of activity. His painful embarrassment at being the only son and thus elected to read the memorial speech. The familiar old stories given a public airing: how the deceased had worked hard all his life, despite ill health, so he could send both his children to college; how he practiced his religious beliefs in his daily life; how they broke the mould after they made him. Tearing up then, snivelling in front of all the old biddies who had been anticipating the moment. *Emmanuel, the son, he was so upset, you know. Broke right down in church. Couldn't even finish the reading.* Subjected to hugs and kisses, pressed into the unyielding corseted bosoms of full-breasted matrons, pats on the back from the men. No time to reflect until later. Years later. But this woman, Anna, was here alone, grieving in silence.

"Why don't you come for dinner tomorrow night?" he invited impulsively. "My wife and I would love to have you. Please," he said. "I've told her so much about your father. I really grew fond of him, maybe because I lost my own father at such a young age. I can't just let him go out of my life, suddenly like this, forever."

For a time she said nothing. He watched her considering him, this foolish man she didn't know, this Emmanuel Taggart whose name and number had appeared repeatedly on the screen of her answering machine, this bumbling, lubberly, middle-aged, balding stranger who, now that her father was dead, was trying to insinuate himself into her life. What was he after?

"All right, Mr. Taggart," she said. "Why not? In

remembrance of my father." She took his measure with cool blue eyes. Exacting.

"Emmanuel. Please. M for short. Your father called me 'Man,'" he chuckled. "Said he couldn't get his tongue around the real name. And my wife is Emily. She's a teacher also. Or, actually, a school counselor. She started back full-time when the boys left. Our sons. We have two. Both in school now. University. The oldest, Gerry, is studying for his Ph.D. in English." He was hot now. His face glowing with perspiration. Once again giving his resume. So she wouldn't feel like she was coming to the house of a complete stranger. "We're in Banbury. Exit 13. 125 Maple Street. It's easy to find. You take a right off the exit ramp and then another right at the third light. We're the fourth house in. On the left. 125. I'll give you my telephone number. Or better yet, I'll call you. To confirm. I know Emily would love to meet you. So it's all settled then?"

He was sweating and stammering like a nervous teenager summoned to the blackboard to execute the equation with red raw hands, to make the negative positive, shuffling up from the back of the room, his face aflame, a continual embarrassing and unwanted bulge in his trousers, trying desperately to remember the formula before he made a complete ass of himself. He had never been good in math.

22

WHAT had he done? He squirmed, hot in his greatcoat, as he drove down the highway toward home. What should he say? How much of his former deception did he have to reveal? Given his wife's generous heart, she would be pleased at his gesture of condolence, he was sure of that. After all, this woman, Anna, had just suffered the death of her father. She apparently had no other family and little opportunity to pursue friendships, being the only caregiver of the debilitated old man for the past number of years. Alone in her grief with no one to comfort her, to share the sorrow. Intolerable! Emily would agree. He'd even consent to summon forth enough energy to clean the house while she was at work, and, under her instructions, would volunteer to prepare dinner. He owed at least this much to the memory of Juhan Lipp.

These reflections awarded him a tiny glow of self regard that he had not experienced for some time now, which dissipated quickly, however, as soon as he arrived home. Restlessly he paced the floor, the words *John is gone, John is gone*, repeating themselves over and over in his brain, until Emily's car finally pulled into the garage.

"John is gone," he told her.

"What?" she said, hanging up her coat in the hallway. "Who?"

"The old man. The old man. I drove to hospital today to see if he was feeling any better – since you suggested I should get out more – and they told me he was gone."

"Gone? Gone where?"

"Gone. Dead and gone."

"Deceased?" asked Emily.

Emmanuel nodded.

"Well, it happens," she said dismissively, heading toward the kitchen to search the freezer for something for supper. "He was very old, wasn't he?" she called back over her shoulder.

He could hardly believe how insensitive his wife had become. Just because a man reached a certain age didn't make his loss any less significant or painful. Ever since Emily went back to work, he had noticed a big change in her. She spent her days compiling checklists that put everyone into neat little boxes, with no allowances made for those who didn't quite fit in. According to her calculations, every single person had to be either this or that. Positive or negative. Straight or gay. Old or young. Happy or sad. Neat and perfect they tried to make life, like a mathematical formula, with everything working out to the preordained conclusion: $x=0$, $y=0$.

Dispassionately he regarded this woman: her blond puffy hairdo, her rounded back and enlarged buttocks as she bent over to put a frozen casserole into the oven. They had argued before, many times, nagged, picked, poked, held each other up to ridicule, broke things along the way, never actually physically abused one another, although they may have felt like it. But it had been self-mutilation, self-hatred. She seemed like a part of himself. Now, for the first time since they met over twenty-five years ago, he saw her as someone altogether separate, someone he no longer knew and was not interested in knowing.

"Don't worry, hon," she said, wiping her hands on the dishtowel. "They wouldn't have a case if they're thinking about suing."

"What?" he said. "Who?"

"The family of the old man. The daughter. The accident. Wasn't he the one you ran into? You said he was confused. Who knows what he told them. You did straighten it out with the insurance company, didn't you, before he died?"

It had gone too far. He was not accustomed to lying. He may have avoided telling the truth on occasion, but he had never falsified directly. Like Mike. *What are you doing?* they would ask him. *Nothin. What are you planning to do? Don't know. What do you want to do? Don't matter. Is something wrong? Don't worry about it.* Gerry was different. They never had to worry about him as much. Maybe because he was the better liar, Emmanuel thought now. Knew how to protect himself more.

"M? Is the insurance taken care of?" Emily persisted.

"Don't worry about it," he said and turned up the TV.

Had it really been only a month since he stumbled from the office, dizzy and weak, dimly aware that his days were numbered? It seemed like years ago when he was still able to pass himself off as just another regular guy: a large, hearty fellow with a bristly red moustache, a glad-hander, a back-slapper, a do-gooder, a man to be counted in, COUNT ME IN, but not someone to be reckoned with or, as it turned out, counted upon. The substance of what he had once been was gone. He had always regarded himself as a good husband and father, a responsible family man. But since they did not need him any longer, what use was he to anyone? There remained nothing to look forward to but the final indignity. To be removed from the world of the living with shit in his diapers. Incinerated. Gone.

Already he had established a new routine: After dinner – which he still picked at like a spoiled child, forcing himself to eat a few bits and pieces in appreciation of Emily's efforts and nagging – he would fall asleep in front of the TV until she went to bed; wide awake then, free to watch sex and violence until the early hours of the morning, when, exhausted, he would climb the stairs to lie down restlessly beside his sleeping wife, the sheets hot and worried, until the alarm got her up and on her way. Only then could he relax, comfortably sprawled across both sides of the bed.

But this morning she tapped him awake.

"I forgot to tell you," she whispered. "I have to stay late at school tonight. Conferences with parents. There are leftovers in the fridge for supper. I'll be home around nine or so."

She kissed her forefinger and pressed it to his cheek. "See you later, hon."

"Mmffhh," he mumbled sleepily, suddenly wide awake as his problem loomed large before his eyes. "Jesus," he sighed through clenched teeth, feeling black clouds gather above him, until he realized that, miraculously, Emily had solved his dilemma without knowing anything about it. She had meetings. She wouldn't be home for dinner. He was sorry, but they both had completely forgotten. There would have to be a change in plans.

Immense relief flooded through his being like a wave

of happiness and he felt a stirring where there had been no signs of life for months. Somewhere he'd heard that men who have sex regularly live longer. A misreading of statistics to be sure. A logical fallacy. Those men were probably healthier to begin with. Still, he thought, there might be something to it. After all, the enormous load of sperm he released must have been stored somewhere. Stagnating. Rotting. Decaying.

Refreshed, he got up earlier than usual. To make arrangements. To develop his strategy. To formulate a compelling story. To call Anna Fedora. What if she didn't believe him? Women were good at "deconstructing the emotional underpinnings." Some psychologist said that on TV and he wondered what that meant exactly. But judging from his own experience with Emily, it had a ring of truth.

Nervous about the task at hand, he consumed three cups of coffee and a large carton of salted cashews to build up his strength for this new regimen of prevarications. Once the cornerstones had been laid, it was almost impossible to change the structure. His only hope was that the foundation remained strong enough to keep the whole fabrication from suddenly falling upon his weak and vulnerable neck.

"Hello, Anna?" he enunciated into the mouthpiece. "How are you feeling today?"

Jovial as a used-car salesman on a slow morning. Not achieving the tone of respectful commiseration he aimed for.

"Yes?" she replied.

Already she could see through him, he could tell by the way she said it.

"Emmanuel Taggart here."

He had to get out of the salesman mode, glad-handing, smiling his phony smile no longer hidden by the moustache, his eager countenance shiny with deception. He had meant to approach her from a position of strength as a man used to dealing with women: a family man, supportive of wife and children; a man with his own office and personal secretary.

"Yes?" she said again.

"I know it's early. I hope I didn't wake you," he apologized.

"No. I'm still in bed, but wide awake."

A momentary vision of Anna Fedora under a white downy duvet, her mass of white hair unfurled upon white feather pillows, her blue eyes open, awake.

"Sorry," he said. "I'm afraid there has to be a change of plans about dinner tonight. I wanted to let you know right away. It's my wife, Emily. She was really looking forward to meeting you, but this morning she remembered she has some sort of a conference tonight. At her school. With parents. She sends her profuse apologies. It completely slipped her mind."

He held his breath.

"Oh, yes?" she said.

He thought she sounded disappointed. Despite his relief that things had worked out so easily, he had to admit he was disappointed himself. Was this to be it then? His memorial to Juhan Lipp terminated so abruptly on the telephone. He felt a compulsion, no, an obligation to do more.

"So how about lunch instead?" he blurted out. Assertive now. A man about town. A man to be reckoned with. "It will just be yours truly, of course, heh, heh. The wife's at work but I really would like to see you again. I'll be there at twelve to pick you up. Okay?"

Silence. Hesitation. Thinking up excuses.

Was he too presumptive? Had he come on too strong? She seemed ethereal to him. Impossible to reach.

"Yes. All right," she said.

A flurry of activity then. An unaccustomed surge of positive energy. The possibility of being of use once again, of trying to cheer someone else on in this difficult game called Life. Juhan's daughter, Anna Fedora. Bearing the mark of his inheritance, there was no doubt about that. Her appraising blue eyes, the reluctant hint of a smile in the corner of her mouth, the mass of pure white hair.

My daughter, Anna, she is a mathematician, Juhan told him. *She likes straight lines and logical answers. She should get out more to see that in the natural world there is hardly a straight line to be found.*

He had expected someone quite different. Older. How old was she anyway? He tried to figure. In her fifties most likely. Ready for early retirement. Now that he was forty-five, that didn't seem quite as old as it had formerly, although he could hardly imagine he himself would soon reach that formidable milestone. Fifty! Half of a whole century! If his disease, whatever it turned out to be, didn't kill him first.

It didn't seem so long ago that he was a teenager and his parents younger than he himself was now. Time really was relative. The fourth dimension. Was that Einstein's big discovery? *It was formerly believed that if all material things disappeared out of the universe, time and space would be left. According to the relativity theory, however, time and space would disappear together with the things.* Einstein himself said that, as a kind of joke to explain his ideas to reporters, Emmanuel remembered reading someplace, though he understood neither the theory nor the joke.

He wished now he had paid more attention to Emily's urgings that he refurbish his wardrobe. His trousers hanging loose. Slim and trim at 195 pounds, though still a bit wobbly in the knees and fuzzy in the head. Perhaps he should take up weightlifting. And certainly he should have made the effort to get the car fixed, the broken headlight and dented fender an unfortunate reminder of the accident and the lies about the insurance, both his own and Juhan's. He would drive her to the city, to a nice restaurant of her choice. Somewhere quiet so they could talk. Because of the special relationship he had with the father, he already presumed an intimate awareness of the daughter, though admittedly somewhat lacking in the particular facts of her existence.

23

"I thought we'd drive to the city," he said. "To a fancy place. Any preference?"

"Your choice," she said, as he helped her with her coat, ran around to open the car door, recalling rusty schoolboy manners from a time when those things were considered a sign of good breeding.

Dressed in black, she looked as elegant as he expected she would. Tall and slender, with just a touch of makeup, her hair done up in the manner of courtly ladies of the Victorian period, with just a few delicate white strands escaping confinement and softening her face. He had a sudden vision of her as a young girl, with her pale long hair, almost white even then, her flawless skin. Self-contained, unapproachable, aloof. Like the Ice Princess in the old Nordic fairy-tale he remembered from childhood, the fame of her beauty bringing suitors from far and wide. But her father, the King, wanted only the best for her. Finally he thought of a plan to test the young men, placing his beloved daughter on the pinnacle of a steep mountain of ice. The man who could reach her and bring her down would have her hand in marriage. Many would try, but all would fail except the one who really loved her.

Was that Fedora? he wondered. And what had happened to him? Juhan had mentioned something disreputable, but what it was? He couldn't quite remember.

"So what brought you out to Summerville in the first place on a collision course with my father?" Anna's voice interrupted his speculations.

Was this a trick question? Did she know? How much had the old man told her? After her initial coldness of the previous day, she seemed now to regard him with the same air of faint amusement as Juhan. Warmly. Fond of the boy, despite his somewhat childish behaviour and immature antics. And as proof of her change in attitude, here she was beside him in the front seat travelling down the empty highway toward the city. He decided to be truthful.

"Well, to tell the truth," he said, "I was lost. Missed my exit. Didn't know where I was. I had the flu or something. Head like a stuffed cabbage. Still recovering, actually. That's why I haven't been at work, if you've been wondering. Thought I'd take a few weeks off and rest up."

He glanced over to see how she was taking this, but her expression betrayed nothing.

"That's why I ran into your father. I wasn't myself. He had his signal light flashing, but I rammed right into him. An unfortunate accident. Then again, I wouldn't have ever met him" – or you, he thought of debonairly adding – "if I'd been more careful. And that would have been my loss."

She looked at him now, considering. He scratched behind his ear, nervous, hoping his story made sense, held together. Surely Juhan had not told her of their ridiculous search.

"And your insurance company is taking care of it then?"

Still worried about the damn insurance. "No, I am. It's just a dent really. Not worth the bother to report."

They sat in silence the rest of the way to the city. He didn't know what to ask her, and she didn't volunteer anything. Still suspicious, obviously, asking about the insurance. Perhaps she thought he was after something – everyone had an agenda – possibly she might be afraid that he had designs on her. A sexual predator perhaps? Yet he had mentioned a wife and kids and knew her father. Besides he hardly seemed the type. Too awkward and clumsy. Too obvious in his bright blue coat. And she certainly was the type of woman who could take care of herself. Another sudden vision of her. In Austria. A bareback rider in the circus: Anna Lipp, her body encased in red sequins, balanced on the broad back of a galloping white stallion, long hair undone, floating out straight behind her.

"Ever been to Pasquali's?" he finally asked as they turned off the exit ramp.

"Actually, yes," she said. "But never for lunch."

"I hear they have wonderful salads," he observed, not knowing what else to say.

When he envisioned this meeting, he couldn't get enough of her. That is to say, he wanted to find out all about her, to probe her soul, to break through her reserve to the real woman beneath. Juhan's daughter, Anna. Someone special in the common denominator of life. He sensed the glow in Juhan's voice whenever he mentioned the name. Yet here they were wasting precious time in silence. It wasn't happening like he'd planned. He almost wished Emily was along tattering about school or children or various female topics to thaw the atmosphere, to break the ice, to get the conversation flowing smoothly.

At the restaurant, he ordered a bottle of wine. "In memory of John Lipp," he toasted. "A remarkable man."

She raised her glass, took a sip and set it down. "What puzzles me," she finally said, "is this strong feeling you seem to have developed for my father in such a short time. Why? A man you ran into in the street, literally. A man you visited a few times in hospital. That in itself surprised me – that you made the effort to go see him – but I attributed it to your concern about the insurance."

Oh-oh, here it comes, Emmanuel thought, suddenly feeling as flat as a glass of stale ginger ale, all his bravado fizzed out of him. This woman, Anna, was a mathematician. She liked to figure things out. She wanted answers. Truth in an epigram, reducing an incredibly long equation to its simplest terms. All thought expressed in numbers. It was the universal language after all. Arriving at proofs that precluded all argument dependent on denotation and connotation or personal preference. What is, is.

Would he be required to reveal all of his dissembling? Even he could see there was an obvious gap in his story, something he hadn't bridged to indicate how he got from there to here. He decided to take a chance. To be honest. To reveal everything and face the consequences. To take it on the chin like a man.

"Well, in actual fact, there was a bit more to it than that," he admitted, rubbing his forefinger across the virginal area that used to bear his moustache. "John and I spent some time together before he had his stroke. At a little restaurant in Dexter. You may know it: The Hungry Horse?"

"Yes?"

"That's all. We just talked. I knew he was hungry for some company and I had nothing to do anyway, being on the sick list, so we got together, that's all."

"To smoke and to drink coffee, I presume?"

"I don't smoke," Emmanuel affirmed.

"I don't mean you. I mean him. I know his bad habits. He was strictly forbidden to even look at caffeine, never mind smoking. That man required constant watching. I even threatened him with a babysitter." She was getting agitated, her hands trembly. "So he was smoking and drinking with you. That explains it!"

"What's that?"

"His stroke. His heart attack. His death. Excuse me," she said and left quickly, taking her purse with her.

Emmanuel remained sitting by himself at the small table upon which the waiter placed two enormous bowls of green salad topped with spiced chicken strips and sprinkled with feta cheese. Was it truly because of his well-intentioned interference that the old man had died? Is that what Anna Fedora thought, weeping now, most likely, in the privacy of the Ladies' Room? Why couldn't he keep his mouth shut? Why did he have to lure an old man to his death with the promise of coffee and cigarettes? I'm sorry. I'm truly sorry. I didn't mean to do it. *By my fault, by my fault, by my most grievous fault,* he watched his father mumble, pounding at his heart with his knuckles, puckering his pious lips to kiss a small cross attached to a necklace of black beads, the rosary. How prissy, he thought then, the few times he had been forced to attend the Catholic Church. Now he wished he himself had some sort of talisman he could supplicate to relieve the guilt in his heart.

He drank some wine to calm himself and absent-mindedly gaped around the room. The restaurant was filled with people, normal people living happy and productive lives, healthy looking people taking a lunch break from the office to fork pieces of lettuce into their mouths, a group of men, executive types, getting up to leave, inadvertently meeting the eyes of one of them, a face slightly familiar. He returned the nod and smile, another huge mistake, for the man took this as an invitation and was heading towards his table. Who was he? Emmanuel recalled a not altogether pleasant encounter. A doctor? A car salesman? Extending his hand.

"How are you, M? Recovered, I trust? Emily with you?" Indicating the empty chair, the untouched salad.

Where had he seen this man before? Something to do with insurance? Then he remembered. Ted, of course. Ted and Lila. The health quacks.

"In remission, actually," he said. That should keep the fellow from prying his nose so casually into other people's business, Emmanuel thought, quite pleased with the reply. Unfortunately, it was just then that Anna decided to emerge from the washroom. Ted looked her up and down with a practiced eye.

"Hello," she said pleasantly, sitting down, none of the emotional distress that Emmanuel had pictured visible on her face. So as not to compromise himself further, he refused to perform the expected introductions. Besides, for the life of him, he could not remember Ted's last name.

"Well, good luck, old chap," Ted said after a moment, slapping him on the shoulder, a vicious smirk lifting up one corner of his mouth, and, Emmanuel was positive, he saw a wink as well. The camaraderie of men about town pursuing their private business.

"Sorry," Anna said. "I didn't mean to lay that on you. It was his own fault, the old sonavabitch. He always was one to break the rules."

Neither of them ate much, and on the drive home they were both silent, preoccupied with their own thoughts.

"Very kind of you. Thank you," she said as he walked her to the door. "It was a lovely gesture. I'm sorry I wasn't quite up for it."

"I'm the one who should be sorry," Emmanuel responded, and he meant it.

That night he told Emily: "I think I should call up the old man's daughter tomorrow. To find out about the funeral plans. Maybe I should go. Feeling a bit guilty. Supposing the accident did have something to do with bringing on the stroke."

"You do what you feel you have to do, dear," she said, giving him a smile of genuine warmth, which left him uncomfortable and itchy for the rest of the evening.

24

IN ordinary circumstances Emmanuel would have soon forgotten about Anna Fedora. After all, he hardly knew her. He had done his duty. He had paid his respects to Juhan. In the grand scheme of things, what did it matter how she regarded him? He would never see her again. But in his present state of agitation, it seemed imperative that he justify his actions and explain himself. In a short while he might exist merely as an imprint in the memories of those who knew him, if they bothered to remember him at all. It was important to leave behind the best picture possible.

Once again he had bungled. *My father never did suffer fools gladly,* she told him. He had managed to redeem himself with the old man, but not with the daughter, for that's exactly how she regarded him now. As a lumbering, self-indulgent fool. Luring the old man into unsavoury adventures with no thought to his health and well-being. Insensitive to her grief. Quite possibly, she even perceived the dinner invitation (so hastily metamorphosed into a lunch date through no fault of his own) as something other than what he meant it to be, viewing it instead as an insidious ploy, a despicable attempt to satisfy some sort of subliminal adulterous longings. Especially if she took note of Ted Whatshisname's conspiratorial wink.

He had to get in touch with her before the weekend, when Emily would be home, fully aware of his every move. With a tremor in his heart, he called the familiar number, hearing the usual click of the answering machine. But then Anna's voice, the real Anna, barely in the nick of time, just like on TV. He hadn't expected her to answer. Wasn't prepared.

"Emmanuel Taggart here," he managed.

There was silence, as she waited.

"What I told you before was all true. But there's more I need to explain. Can I come over?"

How could she refuse a request like that?

Shaking his hand as before. An Estonian custom, he presumed. Something left over from the old country, like the slight trace of accent she still possessed. She led him into the living room this time. Formal. An appointment. To explain himself, like in the confessional. *Bless me, Father, for I have sinned.*

Luckily, he never had been forced into one of those little cubicles. His mother, not being Catholic, didn't believe in it. Religion was always a contentious issue in the family since his father's "return to the faith," as she put it. Although she professed a belief in God and forced her children to go to Sunday school in the Presbyterian church that she sometimes attended, she considered the trappings of the Catholic church as so much mumbo jumbo. A "mixed marriage" it was called in those days. The priest gave them a hard time when they had to get married because Amanda was on the way, or so he gathered from the arguments he had overheard. She was forced to sign a vow to bring the children up Catholic before they were allowed to receive the sacrament of marriage, but his mother never did have any use for the whole lot of them.

"You had something to tell me?" Anna broke into his reverie.

"Oh, yes," he recalled, although faced with her penetrating blue-eyed gaze, this whole mission seemed totally ridiculous. What had possessed him to come here?

"This really has to do with me more than your father," he said.

She gestured slightly with her long fingers, to signal her impatience.

"Okay," he sighed deeply, blowing up a lungful of air to cool off his engorged forehead. "You see, I did get lost like I told you before, but not on the day I bumped into John."

Anna's face remained blank. She was adept at keeping her emotions in check, but he could tell he was beginning to irritate her.

"Actually," he said, "I lost my way a few days before that. Took the wrong exit off the highway, not this one, farther along, out in the country someplace. I was sick, as I told you before. With the flu or something," he added, lest she assume he was a mental patient.

For the second time, he then revealed the entire story of his shameful though innocent dissembling, of eating the dinner prepared for another, of his cowardly retreat, and of his quest to find her again, to make his apologies, for which purpose he had enlisted the aid of Juhan, two old boys on the loose, as it were, with nothing better to occupy their time.

"The old fool," she said when he finished. "He always did have a sense for the absurd."

But she appeared amused and seemed to forgive him, inviting him back then, into the sunny alcove, for coffee. Put a touch of brandy in it for both of them and told him more about her father.

He was born to a prominent family, though not wealthy, for Estonia was a country constantly under siege, occupied by foreign powers: Germans, Swedes, Russians. Juhan's father had been a writer, a poet, a professor, a liberator active in politics and Juhan followed in his father's footsteps. After the First World War there was a brief period of independence in Estonia, a time of great aspiration. That is when he married. A young woman already famous. A musical prodigy. A concert pianist by the time she was twenty. But the good times didn't last before the second war was upon them. Juhan, well known for his anti-Communist views, feared for his life. Along with thousands of others, the young couple fled the country leaving everything behind, not only their families and their material possessions, but all their hopes and dreams as well. They became refugees, displaced persons, part of the nameless horde. When the war ended they were in Austria. It was then they decided to have a child, to begin anew. But a baby wasn't enough. She had lost her reason for being. She never touched a piano again.

"Your father mentioned that," Emmanuel interrupted.

"When we came to this country, I was ready to enter school. They put all their energies into educating me, saving every penny so I could go to university. My father had a job as a school janitor and she worked as a charwoman, her beautiful hands thickened and raw, her spirit broken. She never learned English and began to look upon herself as others saw her – as an ignorant domestic. Only with us could she speak the bitter words that expressed her true feelings, angry that life had cheated her. After a while she turned her face to the wall, and no longer spoke at all. My father was better able to adjust to circumstances. He was still alive, he pointed out, when so many had died. Always he seemed to have the ability to get all he could out of life. Even at eighty-six, when he was supposed to be resting in bed, it appears he was out gallivanting, searching the countryside for a young woman. It was a fitting end. Truly. You gave him the opportunity 'to rage against the dying of the light' as the poet says, despite the constrictions forced upon him by his dutiful daughter."

She turned her head to look out the window.

It was time for him to go. "Thank you," he said. "You have purified my soul." Embarrassed as soon as the hokey words emerged, but she didn't seem to notice.

At the door, she shook his hand again. "Nice to have met you, Emmanuel Taggart. And I'm sure my father felt the same."

He released her hand and gave her a hug. A chaste hug. A bear hug. A tender hug. She felt large in his arms, her body solid through the thick layer of down in his coat, her head level with his own. Different from Emily. He could look down at the top of his wife's head and see the pink of her scalp.

"Take care of yourself now, Anna," he said huskily into the soft cloud of white hair. She had a fresh spring smell about her, not of flowers but of emerging grass. After the rain. This woman. This Anna Fedora.

25

H E felt an almost unbearable sadness on the drive home. For Juhan and his wife. For Anna Fedora. For himself and Emily and their sons, with their major disappointments and tragedies still ahead of them. For all of mankind, in fact, struggling against great odds to find peace and fulfillment.

A vision of Juhan in his study with his books, his writing, his thoughts. Ponderings scrawled upon innumerable legal pads in his nearly illegible handwriting. What was to be done with all this scholarly speculation, these lofty thoughts regarding the nature of man and the Universe, which, in the end, signified nothing? It was his life's work, after all. Revised and revised again. But there was no order to it, no form. The intellectual meanderings of a thinking man. A veritable mountain range of words, reaching great peaks of glory and, at times, plunging into vile depths of the darkest despair. One couldn't just toss it all away, burn it like a pile of trash. "It is thought that makes us human," Juhan said.

An unexamined life is not worth living. Someone famous said that. But so painful to view in its entirety from birth to death, from hopes awakening to hopes extinguished. Emmanuel wiped his hand across his hot forehead, trying to make sense of it all.

He had kept his own life under wraps since his teenage years. Or so it seemed to him now. It was always easier to conform to standard expectations, to pretend to a superficial happiness he didn't really feel, robotically following the path laid out for him by others, day by day, year after year. Even the words that habitually came out of his mouth had made the journey many times before; in fact Emily could finish most of his sentences for him and quite often did just that. He had been sidling through life, scared to look it full in the face, in the back of his mind always the unpleasant aftertaste of an unspecified but persistent guilt. And now it was too late, for it was quite possible he might indeed be dying, no longer in the faraway abstract time but soon. Next year. Next month. Maybe tomorrow. Lying stunned in the hospital bed thinking, is this really all there is. IS THIS IT?

He looked back on his life's journey as if it were a travelogue on TV. Some outstanding moments, yes, a few. Playing street hockey with his best friend, Donny Beener, in the parking lot in back of the church. Their shouts resounding crisply in the cool evening air, the thwack of the puck. In the tree house in summer. Smoking their first cigarettes. Sharing a beer Donny swiped from his Uncle Fred's garage. And later, Bonita, his first love. Wore his class ring around her neck on a chain. A good Catholic girl with black eyes, long lashes, would let him touch and squeeze and suck, but nothing below the waist that she would have to whisper to the priest in the dark confines of the confessional. *Bless me, Father, for I have sinned.* Spending the year with a perpetual hard-on, an ache in his genitals, lover's nuts. What had happened to them all? He hadn't been back since his father's funeral, feeling like a stranger in his hometown, the house sold years before, pieces of furniture he remembered looking out-of-place and shabby in the apartment his parents had moved into when the kids were gone, before his mother left permanently for Florida.

There was a time, he recalled dimly, when he had perceived himself as quite an intellectual. Envisioning his future then, fleetingly, he didn't expect to commute daily from suburbia to sit behind a desk in a small cubbyhole: an easy-going sort, good for a laugh, devoted to his family, no threat to anyone, looked down upon by his wife's newfound professional friends as a harmless bureaucratic booby. In his youth, what lay before him seemed like a vast, amorphous, happily-ever-after time, as he rode off through spacious skies towards a burning sunset with an adoring and beautiful woman by his side. He must have encountered moments of self-doubt and despair on the journey even then, but he couldn't remember any.

As soon as he got home, he dug out an old atlas from the bookshelf and attempted to locate Estonia. For a long time he didn't find it, swallowed up as it was by the huge pink area labelled USSR. He recalled hearing somewhere that after the Communist dissolution some of those small countries got back their independence. He would have to find a newer map.

"So did you go?" asked Emily at supper. Seeing his blank expression, she elaborated. "To the funeral? The memorial service? The whatever? For the old man? What did you say his name was?"

"John. John Lipp."

"From Summerville, did you say? I didn't see anything about it in the obituaries."

"His name wasn't actually John. He was Estonian."

"Oh," she said, concentrating on conducting a forkful of peas into her waiting mouth. "You didn't answer my question."

Blankly he stared at her.

Exasperated, the little m. All the tiny hairs on her body sticking out and quivering with irritation. "For godsakes, M. Are you listening to me? The funeral. Did you attend?"

"They had it already. Yesterday. A small memorial service. Just for the immediate family."

"Oh," she said again, but shot her narrowed-eyes look at him before clearing the dishes and busying herself at the sink.

Later, she read to him from the newspaper: "PSYCHIATRISTS RATIFY S.A.D. GUIDELINES."

"Listen to this: it says here that one in fifty suffer from the condition and the symptoms are 'low energy, trouble concentrating and loss of interest in activities.'" Giving him a meaningful stare after reciting each symptom. "Now here's the good news: it's treatable, it says here, 'by thirty minutes of daily exposure to a light box available commercially for $100 to $500.' You make sure, M, that you tell that specialist everything on Monday. It wouldn't be a bad idea to make a list of your symptoms. Maybe I should take the day off and go with you."

Another tribulation! He'd forgotten all about this latest appointment.

"Not necessary for you to go, Emily. I'm a big boy now," he said rather curtly but refused to feel badly about it. After all, it was he who was suffering.

26

THE examination was cursory, but he was convinced now that he was dying.

Meticulously he had listed all his symptoms as Emily had suggested, worrying anew about each one: weight loss, lack of appetite, diminished energy, a ringing in his ears, a feeling of detachment, dizziness, fatigue, sleeplessness, the perpetual sense of doom which sometimes caused his heart to palpitate and a cold sweat to form on his brow and elsewhere.

"Have I left anything out?" he asked his wife.

"Mood swings," she added, "irritability, lack of testosterone."

But Dr. Acton, the Specialist, preoccupied with his file, did not seem at all interested in this painstakingly composed list, nor even in the actual fact of his person. A nattily dressed, dark-complected fellow with a British accent, he looked more like a businessman than a doctor.

At least Emmanuel was not subjected to the same indignities as before. Dr. Acton merely reached around from his polished desk to listen to his heart, examine around his throat with manicured fingers and beam a piercing light into both his eyes, declaiming "ahum,

ahum," all the while, his breath stinking of mouthwash. Further tests were needed, he said, recommending a CAT scan. Or, better yet, an MRI.

"Don't want to worry you unnecessarily, Emmanuel, but with your symptoms, there are all sorts of possibilities. It's better to be safe than sorry, eh? Nothing to concern ourselves about yet. Not until we know for sure. Righto! My receptionist will make all the necessary arrangements. She'll call you."

There was not one thing in the least reassuring about this. They wanted to see his insides. They wanted to check out his brain. Something serious, perhaps even terminal, was wrong with him. According to the specialist, there were all sorts of possibilities to choose from. This was no longer a joke. A hollow feeling in the pit of his stomach. But he had to accept the facts. Everyone who is born, dies. The simple equation of life: $0 = 0$.

Yet oddly enough, he felt strangely elated as well. The touch of Death upon his brow gave him an importance he had been lacking for some time now. It was, after all, just as significant as one's birth. A flurry of preparations long before the anticipated event. Whispered confidences. *Oh yes, it's terminal. He's taking it well, with his chin up, although his family is finding it difficult, as can be expected.* Readjustments in the lives of his loved ones. Travel plans made. His sons hurrying home. Amanda and her family coming from Florida. Would his mother be able to make the trip? he wondered. They would all rally behind him with a religious service replete with speeches and tears and a nice lunch of little sandwiches and squares afterwards. May he rest in peace.

Since he was already in the city, he briefly considered presenting himself at his office now that certain things had been confirmed. *Been to a specialist. Waiting for an MRI. They think it may be something in the brain.* Rose's eyes and lips rounding into sympathetic O NO's. But then he decided against it. Already he would be a stranger, not fitting in, no longer privy to the current gossip, standing around like a fifth wheel while the bureaucratic machine continued to putter along without him. Soon they would forget him entirely, the plastic sign proclaiming his existence remaining on his office door due to a shortage of custodial services, some other man sitting behind his desk shuffling papers, depending on Rose to do what needed to be done.

Stopped at a coffee shop instead to collect his thoughts. *Just waiting for someone,* in case anyone asked. *Guess she got delayed, stuck in traffic, forgot the time, stood me up, heh heh.* Leaving a sizeable tip, the big spender, the man-about-town. Beating a quick retreat. After downing three large mugs of coffee, his teeth on edge from all the caffeine, he realized he couldn't very well go back inside to use the washroom. Walking the streets, in desperate need now, the pain in his bladder convoluting the muscles of his face. A Letter to the Editor demanding public urinals. Protesting at the Town Hall, waving large placards and chanting WE GOTTA GO.

At last, an alleyway. He should have listened to Emily and chosen a coat of a more subdued colour less obvious in the dim shade among back doors and garbage cans. Still, a man's gotta do what he's gotta do. Against the wall. How high can you shoot? How long can you dribble? He would have won all the old boyhood contests. Stepping out, relieved, feeling the sunshine upon his face, a new man. Ready to face the future and whatever it might bring. The common little things, really, turned out to be the most important in the end.

Emily was already home when he got there. Tore into him like a yappy chihuahua before he even got his coat off. "Where have you been, Emmanuel? I've been going crazy wondering about you. Called at noon. No answer. Thought you must still be at the doctor's so I pretended sudden illness, took the rest of the day off, drove over there but you had left long ago. Called home again. No answer. I've been here for two hours pacing the floor."

"I went for a coffee," he said lamely. "Walked around."

"Why didn't you call me? You said you would phone right after you found out the diagnosis and leave a message. I've been worried sick, for godsakes. Thought you might have gotten yourself lost again," she said to punish him.

"There was no diagnosis."

"Well what did the specialist say, Emmanuel? He must have told you something? What's wrong with you?"

A brain aneurysm. Possibly. He could blow the lid right off her pot by telling her that. But it would leave her simmering and she'd pay him back thousand-fold by the time it was all over.

"He looked me over for about three minutes and couldn't find a thing. Scheduled some tests, that's all."

"What kind of tests?"

"CAT scan. MRI."

"Oh, M," she wailed, stricken. "They must think it's serious then."

Almost, she had made him feel sorry for his callous manner, but that did it!

"You think I'm making it all up? That I'm really fit as a fiddle, ready to hop to it and play a jig? What you really believe is that I'm a slacker, a hypochondriac, a person who's SAD and needs a five-hundred dollar lit-up box to make him happy. Or maybe some naturopathic folderol from your homeopathic friend, dapper Ted? Honestly, Emily, I thought you were with me in this, sympathetic at least, but now you're sounding as though this is all pretence on my part, some sort of psychological game I'm playing. It's because of those damn forms you're diddling with all the time. They give you the wrong perspective of what life is really about."

A pit bull on the attack. He was not about to allow anyone to yap at him, even in his weakened condition. He'd give her the what-for!

But this time, he'd gone too far. Emily stood with her mouth open like a drowning fish before running upstairs, snivelling. For a short while, Emmanuel fumed on in the living room, but then, contrite, went to apologize.

She was lying on the bed, sobbing into the pillow. He sat down beside her, rubbed her back, handed her a box of tissues.

"I'm sorry, Emily," he said. "It's all this pressure in my head. I don't know what comes over me." He could have mentioned a brain tumour now to excuse himself, but he did feel genuinely bad about his vile behaviour and didn't want to worry her further.

"I do believe you," she said, blowing, her face red and swollen. "Of course I believe you. Look at you. You're half the size you used to be a few months ago." She managed a rueful little smile. "It's like going to bed with a stranger. I'm just trying not to imagine the worst."

But later, he caught her staring. "Is there something you're not telling me?" she asked.

"We just have to wait and see," he said. "No sense getting all riled up until we know what's what."

Sleepless, the Big M. Worried about the mysterious convolutions of his brain. The unknown spots. The ones they had to check.

Donny Beemer's father had died of a brain tumour, when they were both about fifteen and life presented an endless panorama of change with periods of unrelieved boredom in between. The old man was late coming home from work one night and called his wife from a phone booth somewhere in the next county. Didn't know where he was. Still remembered his own name, but had to look up his telephone number. Things regressed quickly. They shaved off his massive Afro and operated on his brain. But it was too late. Donny changed after that. Quit the basketball team. Didn't hang around with the boys anymore. Didn't talk about it, even to Emmanuel. The family may have moved, he couldn't recall.

It was a good thing his boys were older, off on their own now when this was happening to him. They still asked for money but there would be the life insurance. His mortgage was paid. Both cars were financed, though he had made sure they got the extra insurance in case of death or disability. He had a pretty good benefit plan from work: medical insurance, funeral expenses, a pension for the widow. Emily would be financially secure. As for his funeral, he would prefer to be cremated with no fuss or muss. If they wanted to have some sort of private memorial ceremony for the family, it would be up to them. At that point, he would be beyond caring.

These thoughts calmed him. He hadn't done so badly after all. Ready to go, was Emmanuel, when the big summons came. His affairs, most of them, were in order.

27

L IKE a light that burns more brightly for a brief instant before being extinguished forever, Emmanuel regained some of his life energy. The cards had been dealt. All he could do now was to play out the game as best he could. He turned off the talk shows and fluffed up the pillows of the davenport. He carried out the garbage, vacuumed the house, made the bed. He arranged for an appointment to have his car repaired. He telephoned his sons to let them know how desperately he missed them, choked up thinking he might never see them again. First speaking to Gerry's answering machine: "How's it going? Everything okay? Just thought I'd check in to see how you were doing." Then to Mike's: "How's it going? Everything okay? Just thought I'd check in to see how you're doing." I'M LEAVING, I'M HALF GONE ALREADY, SO YOU'LL HARDLY NOTICE WHEN I DISAPPEAR. He called his mother in Florida, and his sister Amanda. GOODBYE, SO LONG, IT'S BEEN NICE TO KNOW YOU.

I'M DYING YOU KNOW, he felt like shouting to strangers. Soon he would no longer be in this house, on this street, in this town, on this earth, his particular and unique consciousness reuniting with the amorphous mass. He went for a walk, stopping on the sidewalk in full view of everyone to watch a bunch of crows at his neighbours' bird feeder. Apprehending Creation. Even now he could feel the tumour becoming larger, growing tentacles, creeping along the convolutions of grey matter inside his skull, causing power surges, short circuits, blackouts. But while his lights were still flickering, he would make the most of it. His brain waves, frothy with foam, crashed ashore, dispersing piles of refuse which had accumulated over the years, and Emmanuel strode manfully through the bracing spray, red-faced and puffing with exertion, aware, finally, that the rest of his life had arrived.

For a reason he couldn't quite define, it seemed imperative that he see Anna Fedora one last time. To say goodbye. To reconfirm his brief existence in another sphere entirely, different from the one in which he normally dwelled. To let her know that the memory of her father would help him get through this. She might not be over-joyed to find him on her doorstep, but she would probably invite him in.

"Going for a drive," he called to his wife on a Saturday morning. "To clear my head."

He could tell she wanted to come along to keep an eye on him, but was too intimidated to say so. During the past few days he had almost been like the man she remembered, she told him, and she was obviously being extra careful not to breathe on the kindling and flare up the temper. If he needed to clear his head, then so be it.

"Be careful, hon," she said, kissing her finger and pointing it at him. "I think I'll go out myself. Do some shopping."

Emmanuel Taggart heading north, toward the white house of Anna Fedora, preparing his introductory speech. What could he say about so suddenly reappearing? What excuse could he make? He probably should have called first to make an appointment: *I need to see Ms. Fedora on urgent personal business. No, I can't wait, I'm dying.* He tried to imagine Anna's life, the part he didn't know. Brilliant, studious, a scholarship student. A math major. In his adolescent world, girls like that didn't have to be reckoned with. Wearing horn-rimmed glasses and dowdy skirts, they moved on another plane from his entirely. But Anna was different. Beautiful and distant, with that northern reserve which kept suitors at bay. Yet she had been married. To a cad, apparently. Asshole Fedora.

Walking to her door, he felt like he was still in junior high, awkwardly making the interminable trip across the gym floor to ask a girl to dance. She could see right through him, this Anna Fedora, he was sure of it, and she knew better than he himself what lay within the deepest recesses of his heart. Ringing the doorbell, tapping his heel impatiently on the doormat, pushing the buzzer again, relieved that no one answered.

What exactly was he doing here? What could he possibly say had she opened the door? Nothing seemed suitable. Still, he made his way back to the car like an old hound with his tail between his legs, having lost the scent, and decided to cheer himself up with a cup of coffee at the restaurant he and Juhan had patronized together.

"Hi there," said the waitress, recognizing him. "Your father not with you today?"

"Not today," he replied. That seemed easier than attempting to clarify the situation to a stranger who was merely trying to be polite.

Sitting in the same booth, conjuring up the old man opposite him, his quirky pink-cheeked visage, his blue eyes, like Anna's, regarding him with indulgence and good humour. Juhan seemed to have found the answers to the great mystery of life, whereas he himself had not taken the time even to ask the questions. *We can be knowledgeable with other men's knowledge but we cannot be wise with other men's wisdom,* some philosopher remarked centuries ago. These days they were trying to pass wisdom around like teacakes. Self-improvement manuals sold by the millions, the authors pontificating on morning talk shows, their pockets stuffed with easy cash.

Emmanuel fumed silently into his coffee. Soon he too would exist only as a remembrance in the minds of those who had known him, the shape of his energy field exuding from places he had frequented: his desk in the office, behind the wheel of his car, lying on the sofa with his remote control, on the left side of the bed he and Emily shared. Already he had slipped out of their lives, only the thought of him remaining like the indentation of his body permanently pressed into the mattress he had slept on for twenty-odd years. They would miss him, yes, but only if they stopped to think about him. Emily more than the boys, accustomed to the daily routine, his toothbrush next to hers in the holder. She would weep, folding his clothes into boxes for the Goodwill – Emmanuel almost brought to tears himself envisioning the moment – his little wife desolate among his things, sniffing the clothes he had recently worn to inhale once more his familiar smell. But all too soon the new would replace the old – not actually replace it as much as push it into the background, overcome it, until that which used to be remained only a hazy image on the horizon of her life. She had her sons, her friends at work, the job itself which demanded so much of her time and which she found so fulfilling. She would be financially secure, almost wealthy, selling the house, moving into a small apartment in the city, closer to the school. Why were they keeping their house in the suburbs anyway, now that the boys were gone? Neither of them enjoyed mowing the lawn. It didn't make sense for the two of them to live in such a big place for the few occasions they might have guests staying overnight. Three spare bedrooms so they could accommodate non-existent grandchildren. He would mention it to Emily. There might be a bit of time left yet to function in the foreground.

Rejuvenated by these thoughts, Emmanuel drove by Anna's house once again. He could tell she had returned. He sensed her energy emanating from within like a glow of warmth from a fired-up stove. Besides, her car was in the driveway.

"Hi," he said when she answered the door.

She didn't smile, but did open the door wider to let him in. Her hair pulled together, hanging down her back.

"I was in the neighbourhood," he explained, "so I thought I'd drop by to see how you're making out."

"Still on the search?" Smiling at him at last. His knees weakened with relief. She was going to allow him to stay.

"Does your wife know about this visit?" she asked when they had settled themselves at the kitchen table.

"Actually, no," said Emmanuel. "I don't want her to get the wrong idea. She tends to be the jealous type."

"I see," said Anna, a glint of amusement appearing in her eyes. "And what sort of idea is that?" Wanting to see him squirm, watching to see him wiggle out of this one.

"She's of the old school," he said. "Thinks that a man and a woman can't be just friends."

"I see," she said again. "And have you ever been 'just friends' with a woman?"

"Of course," he justified himself. "My colleagues at work. My secretary, Rose."

"And do you visit them often?"

"No," he admitted, "but there is absolutely no reason that I shouldn't."

"I don't mean to put you on the spot, Emmanuel," she said, "but I've been on my own long enough by now to be familiar with the behaviour of men. Are you having trouble with your relationship at home or are you hoping for something new on the side?"

He wasn't expecting this. What was she thinking? That he was here to take advantage? His few previous half-hearted attempts with women had always been conducted in the shade, the stark outlines softened by shadows, by a few drinks, by insinuations, sometimes by outright lies. Now his motives were being probed and examined in the bright glare of reality and he wasn't sure he could withstand it. Anna had warned him. *I like things to be neat and tidy,* she said. *I like problems to have solutions.*

"No, no," he defended himself. "It's not like that at all. I mean, you are a very beautiful woman, of course, but what I need is to talk to you," he said. "You remind me of John."

"In that case," she laughed, "we have nothing to worry about. Would you like a drink? I usually indulge myself this time in the afternoon."

"I feel close to you already, having met your father. But I want to know more about you. As a person. And as a woman. And also I want to reveal myself to you. As I am. As I want to be. I'm finally willing to take the chance and do what my own impulses tell me.

I've lived my entire life thus far trying to fulfill the expectations of others; now I want to do what's right for me. Is that so wrong? The truth is, I am facing my imminent death," Emmanuel babbled, the large drink of Jack Daniels on ice coursing rapidly through his arteries and directly into his starved brain, causing a sudden squall of considerable proportions.

"You look like you have a few good years left in you yet," she remarked. "Of course, I am used to sitting across this table from my father."

Should he tell her the truth?

"I have been ill, you know. I haven't been myself since the beginning of February. They aren't quite sure what it is yet, the doctors. Not definitely."

"Do you feel sick now?"

"No. I feel great. Drunk, I think, actually."

"Well then, why despair? We're all under the same sentence of death after all. It's one of the axioms of life. Positive, negative. Plus, minus. Yin, yang. I hoped to become a mathematician before Fedora got in the way. Mathematicians speak the universal language in its purest form, and logic is the hygiene to keep one's mind healthy and strong."

"I was always inferior at math," Emmanuel sheepishly admitted. "Could never figure out when Car A started at point B at a velocity of 50 miles per hour, and car C started at point D at 80 miles per hour, exactly how long it would take before they crashed. And to tell you the honest truth" – he grinned – "I didn't give a damn."

Anna Fedora allowed him a dimple.

He basked in the warmth of her look, glowing from within like a Christmas candle. Or then again, perhaps the glow was due to the whiskey he had consumed.

"Mathematics searches for truth in its most basic form. All natural phenomena and every single physical process are governed by laws, and those laws can be described by mathematical equations. My father was rather intolerant of this view. He looked upon the entire discipline as a narrow construction. It is impossible for man to understand the totality of existence, he believed; he can merely apprehend it. Mathematics may affirm truths, he said, but it negates life.

"I suppose I took after my mother," she continued after a brief silence, both of them sipping at their drinks. "I had the same sort of fascination for the precision of numbers as she found in music. And approached it with equal passion, I might add. But you can only do that when you're young, before life gets in the way."

She got up then and took their empty glasses to the counter. Didn't offer him a refill. How did your life get in the way? he wanted to ask, but she might think he was prying. He was grateful she had revealed this much. She had at least admitted him into the presence of her mind, if not her soul. He glanced at his watch. It was getting late. Emily would be wondering about him. He'd have some explaining to do.

"You better have a coffee before you go," she suggested. "We don't want your other headlight banged up as well."

But he was fine. The sudden gale had abated. The seas were calm once more. The skies had lightened.

At the door she extended her hand and he took it. "Take care of yourself, Emmanuel," she said.

28

"**D**o you think your parents have always been eccentric, or did they become that way in their old age?" Emmanuel asked his wife.

"What?" Emily laughed.

She barely glanced at him, keeping her eyes firmly on the road, her hot hands gripping the steering wheel, a careful driver of the inside lane, her foot anticipating the brake, always ready for the unexpected. It drove him crazy. But they had to take her car because his smashed headlight had yet to be fixed. And because of his infirmity, she insisted, martyr-like, on driving herself. These little foreign cars that women loved! Uncomfortably he shifted in the hard seat, his back sore, his neck stiff.

"When people get old everyone assumes they get weird," he continued. "My point is this: have they always been that way, but when they were younger, no one noticed?"

He glanced at Emily to see how she was taking this. Her lips perked up slightly but she said nothing. Too busy driving. It took a lot of prodding to get her growling these days, her patient endurance of his mysterious infirmity irritating him further. She had been extra nice to him ever since his appointment with the specialist. Accommodating. So as not to ruffle his brief re-emergence, not as himself perhaps, but as a do-gooder somewhat in his father's mould. He could feel his better nature beginning to wear thin, however, peeling off his backside even now. In fact, he was itching to pick a fight so he could blame someone for something. Cruel and disloyal. Yes, and angry. Didn't he have the right, deprived as he was of his natural life expectancy? Mowed down before his time? Before he could gather a cloak of wisdom around himself to cushion the end.

"There's not a group of people more cowed into conforming than the old. You can't get away with anything once you reach a certain age. Why should all old men have to wear baggy trousers, get their nose hairs clipped, the back of their neck shaved every three weeks, and drink cupfuls of tea? Answer me that!"

"Because they want to?" she said in a pretentiously tiny voice, not sure how to respond to this outburst.

"Let's face it, Emily. If they don't, they're considered crazy old coots."

"My parents haven't changed at all, really, I don't think," she ventured.

"My point exactly!" Emmanuel raised his index finger. "They didn't seem totally weird when they were younger, but now they do. We notice their eccentricities more. It's because of our perception of what all old folks should act like."

"Yours maybe," said Emily, becoming testy. "I don't find them strange at all."

He never should have agreed to this trip. *A day trip*, she called it, *it'll be good for you, M, to get out. It's supposed to be a sunny day, and we didn't get to go at*

Christmas. Planning and conniving. Manipulating her weakened spouse to get her own way. Three hours to get there and three to get back, with her driving. A torture session stuck in this bucket seat manufactured for Japanese asses smaller than his. He was definitely not well, scheduled for a major assessment. Her sympathy, obviously, was wearing thin.

But now that he considered further, his sudden illness was probably the real reason for the journey in the first place. Everyone has a hidden agenda. Emily on the telephone to her mother. Attempting to reassure them. Proving the fact by showing him off. *See, here he is in the flesh!* A smaller and nastier version than they might remember, but it's him nevertheless, the Big M, standing on his own two feet! *Hello there, Mom,* bending down to give the little woman a hug, maybe for the last time. Winnie insisted on being called "Mom," but he could never imagine calling old Abelard "Dad." *Abe is good,* his new father-in-law had said gruffly.

It was not hard to tell that Abe never liked him. *What do you do then,* he asked when Emily first brought him home…*"M"? I work for the city,* he answered, *for the Planning Commission. I mean, what work do you do?* he asked, eyeing Emmanuel suspiciously. Emily intervened. *He's got a very important job, Dad. Every form that comes in or goes out of that office requires his signature.*

They had seemed old to him even then, Emily's parents. Like his own did. In their late forties, he judged. Just marking time before the final good-byes. But they hadn't seemed particularly odd. Not *really* eccentric, like they appeared to him now. It was true, what Emily said. They hadn't changed at all. They hadn't altered their lifestyle like they were supposed to as they hit that certain milestone called Really Old, when saying *We're getting old*, was followed by a sigh rather than a chuckle. Abelard, in dirty striped coveralls, coming in from outdoors for his dinner, leaving his muddy work boots on the mat, entering the hot kitchen which always smelled of vinegar and spices where Winnie – "Mom" – spent her life chopping fruits and vegetables into small squares for chow, for relishes, for jams, for preserves, for pies, for hodgepodge, to freeze and can. Washing his dirty hands in the kitchen sink. *That man!* she would exclaim in exasperation, rolling her eyes up to heaven, *We got indoor plumbing years ago and he still pees in the yard.* But she would never complain if Abe was anywhere within hearing distance.

"You know those coveralls your father wears?" asked Emmanuel. "Do you suppose they're the same ones he had on when I first met him?"

"Surely not!" Emily replied, amused by the thought, but he could tell she wasn't certain.

Emily was a "farm girl," or that's what she called herself. *I'm just a farm girl*, she'd say, *what do I know?* every time it became obvious that she had the upper hand in an argument and he was being obstinate by not agreeing with her. Actually, although her parents did live out in the sticks, they never really owned what could be considered a farm. A small barn, acres of woodland where Abe hunted and cut down trees for firewood, an enormous vegetable garden, fruit trees, berry bushes, all sorts of animals at one time or another. He remembered a brown cow tethered in the front yard eating dandelions, a pig in the back eating garbage, a couple of sheep eating the grass which Abe refused to mow, an old workhorse in the barn used for hauling logs out of the forest, hens roosting in the trees around the house, ducks and geese in the pond, countless cats, various dogs, tame crows, a raccoon that had become vicious and tried to drag Winnie into the woods – Abe showed him the pelt – rabbits in wire cages, pet squirrels, and more he couldn't specifically recall. Abelard worked as a school bus driver, but did a lot of other things on the side.

Emmanuel closed his eyes and turned on the radio. It was useless to get any conversation out of his wife when she was busy driving. A rockabilly whining a lover's lament: *Thar's a hole in my heart where you usta be, that can only be filled by you.* The lyrics made his heart ache so that his eyes teared up under his closed lids. What had happened to the life he used to have that he took so much for granted? His sons, his beautiful boys, gone. Clean and rosy, their soft blond hair still damp from the bath, clothed in identical flannel pyjamas, they would cuddle in his lap as he read to them from *Winnie the Pooh*. Sniffling loudly, he could feel Emily's sharp look: *he wasn't getting a cold, was he, on top of everything else?*

They were off the highway now, driving over potholed blacktop, winding toward the gravel road which would bring them to their destination. Once the boys grew up, they didn't make this trip very often, and Abe and Winnie never came to the city. In the first place, their car probably wouldn't make it; and secondly, Abelard refused to go anywhere if it was not absolutely necessary. Ever since Emmanuel had known them, he had driven a succession of elderly vehicles, for it was Abe's firm conviction never to buy a new car. *You lose a thousand bucks when you drive it offa the lot, for chrissakes. Buy an old one for that amount and you can still getta few good years outta her.* Various rusting hulks stood guard in the back of the house by the barn; others, Emmanuel knew, had made it to the high bank on the far side of the property to be dumped overboard.

Even when the boys were young, the Taggarts didn't spend much time at the "farm." When they were little, they were terrified of the animals: the crow that would land on their unsuspecting heads, the pig that rooted up the rotting fence of his pen and ran freely around the yard eating apples in the orchard, the enormous horse with the nibbly nose baring its long brown teeth, the bear Abe had seen in the back woods. Grampa's stories at the dinner table didn't help. *That city life is turning them lads into sissies,* Abe would grumble. When they were older, it was the neighbour boy they were afraid of. *He's got a gun, Ma, and no teeth,* Gerry whined. *He tortures little animals and he shoots chickens out of trees with a bow and arrow. He's mean, Ma.* Inside the house there was nothing to do. The grandparents had no TV.

"There you are!" said Winnie, "Finally!"

Standing on the doorstep, wiping her hands on a dishtowel, Fender beside her wagging his meagre tail, too old now to bark. The smell of good home cooking wafted out of the open door into the front yard, meat and potatoes, for that's the kind of man she married.

"Dad's out back piling wood," she said. "He'll be in for his dinner soon."

Hugs and kisses all around. Emmanuel thoroughly scrutinized, but Winnie forewarned by her daughter not to say anything even remotely related to the topic of health, not even a *how-are-you*, nervously grimacing at her daughter, raising her eyebrows, squeezing out the corners of her mouth, waggling her head like a chicken. She was even smaller than Emily, or perhaps she had shrunk. Blown aloft by a strong gust of wind in the supermarket parking lot just last month, Emily had told him, scraped up a bit when she landed.

Inside, the house smelled the same, the aroma of vinegar and spices soaked into the floorboards, the walls. From the kitchen window they could see Abelard in his striped coveralls and knitted toque, piling small pieces of kindling neatly on a large circular woodpile resembling a yurt. Several other yurts stood already completed in the backyard.

"He likes to keep busy," Winnie said, wiping her hands again. "In for his dinner, and then outside again until it gets too dark to do anything. Come, come, children. You must be exhausted after the long drive, my dear girl."

Winnie pretended to be nice, but deep in her heart she resented him for taking their only child so far away. Making her get a job. Making her drive all that way because her citified husband was too sick with some sort of mysterious ailment to take care of her properly. Winnie herself never did get a driver's license. Like a proper husband, Abelard took her everywhere she had to go, waited in the car until she was done. She took a good long look at this son-in-law she was stuck with, up and down, her mouth stretched to its limit, her head waggling.

"Something to drink? I've got fresh pop."

There really wasn't much to talk about, with the topic of health off limits and Emily dutifully gabbling on the phone with her mother every other day, giving her the latest news. Old Fender came over to sniff at Emmanuel's pant leg, displaying a huge lump on the side of his neck and exuding a vile doggie smell. He could see Winnie wanting to discuss the lump, but she didn't dare.

"Dad didn't get a deer this year," she said. "But he's been snaring rabbits regular. That's what we're having. You sure you won't have something to drink? I've got fresh pop."

The thought of a recently killed bunny did nothing to improve Emmanuel's appetite. Emily's parents had always been heavy on the meat – fresh venison, fresh pork, slabs of freshly butchered beef, spring lamb, roosters shot out of the trees that very morning, duck, partridge, geese, plucked by Winnie before she threw them into the cooking pot. But when he had pointed this out to Emily, she grew indignant. *Do you think he kills those animals for his own pleasure like those weekend hunters who fly to Newfoundland to shoot the last remaining caribou? We had to eat, you know. He did the best he could.* Emmanuel admired her loyalty and felt guilty about his ambivalent feelings toward his own family. Maybe he was incapable of deep, true, abiding, real love. But why? *You don't love anybody but yourself,* Emmanuel. Had someone said that to him? He couldn't remember.

29

PRICKLY, the Big M, on the drive home, a porcupine lodged in his brain and the rabbit still hopping around in his stomach. Tried his best with the stew, but halfway through had to excuse himself, thankful for the indoor plumbing.

"Got the grippers, boy?" Old Abe grinned, when he finally emerged, dessert on the table, only Emmanuel's dinner plate remaining.

"Apple and rhubarb pie," Winnie coaxed. "Hope you made room."

"I'm sorry," he said. "I just can't."

Always, Winnie served food as if to the starving – *More, have more, there's a lot here yet, vegetables are good for you, sure you won't have any more? Gotta eat up or tomorrow won't be a sunny day* – but obviously Emily had done some conferencing while he was absent. They scrutinized him with pity and accepted his excuse.

When he finished his pie, Abelard pushed back the chair, winked at Emmanuel and, raising up his grizzled maw, pointed it towards the door. This was the signal to put on their coats and boots and go outside. While the women cleared up and washed the dishes, the men would sit in the newest of the old cars. There Abe produced a bottle of brandy and two shot glasses.

"This will fix 'er," he said, tipping back his head, neatly emptying the little glass in one gulp. "Echhhh!" he sputtered. "How about another?"

Emmanuel had participated in this ritual before. Abe brought out the bottle whenever there was company, but only men were invited to indulge. Although it was cold outside in the car, the liquor warmed their innards and they sat for quite awhile staring at the woodpiles in the back yard.

"Yep," Abe said. "That wood is nice and dry. Should keep us warm next winter."

Then they went back inside.

It was obvious that mother and daughter had a chance for an intimate tête-à-tête while he was away, for Winnie was more frazzled than usual, teary-eyed, squeezing her lips together to press down the corners, puffing out sighs like a steam engine. When they were leaving, she took both his hands in hers.

"Take care of yourself now, dear," she said, squeezing hard, the tears starting to flow.

"I will, Mom, don't you worry," he assured the old woman, giving her a hug. She had shrunk. She felt like a small child in his arms.

"Goodbye," Abelard harrumphed, settling himself down in his recliner.

"Goodbye, old Fender," said Emmanuel, but didn't touch the dog or he would have to go back and wash his hands.

Winnie waving from the doorstep as Emily warmed up the car. Wiping her eyes with the dishtowel.

Life was so sad, reflected Emmanuel as they drove away down the gravel road. He felt like weeping himself, but the pain in his gut retarded sentimentality. Three hours to go before the comfort of his own shithouse. He wasn't sure he could make it.

"How about a coffee?" Emily said, pulling into the Irving station by the highway. "I could use one."

When Emmanuel emerged from the bathroom, she was settled into a booth and decided she might have a ham sandwich as well. He couldn't believe it. How could she eat after just having consumed an enormous dinner?

"That was hours ago," she said. "It's suppertime now."

Shaking his head in disbelief, he nevertheless volunteered to go to the counter and get it for her. After all, she was the one driving.

"Toasted or untoasted?" asked the girl.

"Just a second," Emmanuel said, "it's for my wife."

"White or whole wheat?"

"One moment," said Emmanuel.

"Mustard?"

"Jesus!" said Emmanuel as he walked to the booth at the back of the restaurant a third time.

"Pickles?"

"Give it everything you've got," he said to the girl. "And I'll have a small coke."

Obviously irritated, the girl shoved over the sandwich and an empty plastic cup.

"What's this?" Emmanuel inquired, turning the cup upside down and shaking it.

"Wasn't it a small coke you wanted?" she snarked at him and turned away to serve another customer.

Fuming black smoke, he brought Emily's sandwich to the table. "I can't believe this place," he said, displaying his cup. "It's empty."

"See that machine over there?" His wife pointed. "You get your own."

He felt the girl's eyes upon him as he read the directions on the machine. A rube from the sticks obviously, untutored in the ways of the modern world. No wonder Abelard didn't travel far from the "farm." There, he was king of his domain. Here, he would be regarded as a bumbling old fool. "Holy snappin arseholes," he remarked loudly, in deference to his father-in-law, that being one of his common expressions.

The rest stop did nothing to improve his mood. Emily better keep her foot even closer to the brake. There was danger ahead. The porcupine was raising its quills. But he was too tired to start anything. Just groaned a lot and belched and farted a few times to ease his indigestion.

"Heavens to Betsy, M, what a stink!" Emily complained taking her hand off the steering wheel long enough to waft it about in front of her face and open the window, letting in a blast of cold air.

"Whose idea was it to take this so-called day trip anyway?" he responded. "You'll just have to suffer the consequences, my dear."

The fresh air revived him, unfortunately, to begin another monologue. "Family," he said. "What is it really except a collection of people who are forced to think nicely about one another when they're far apart, but find being together quite intolerable really. You've got to admit, Emily, today was a total disaster, to be added to the long list of previous visits just as horrible. Did any of us really enjoy ourselves? Family obligation, that's all it is. And it's not just your folks, Em, don't get me wrong. Remember our last trip to Florida to visit Mom? My Mom? Just think back to all the complaining you did about those beautiful days wasted walking around shopping malls because those women cared nothing about lying on the beach and didn't give a hoot about what you wanted to do. Don't deny it. You hated it. *Waste of time and money*, you said. Then there's our two boys. Of course we love them, they're our sons, we did the best we could for them – we're still doing it. But do they ever think about us? When I talked to Mike last week, he asked for money for his March break trip, but after that we had little to say to one another. What I mean, Em, is this: basically, the only person we spend our entire life with is ourselves. And we should remember that fact. After all, life is short and death is long, as they say. The present moment is all we've got."

Emily maintained a stony silence throughout this spiel, staring straight ahead at the road, her lips compressed. Beginning to look a lot like her mother, Emmanuel appraised, glancing over at her, especially if she lost some weight and let her hair go grey. Perhaps it was grey already, who could tell, with all that gunk she put in it to make herself appear younger.

"You've gotten to be a right selfish sonavabitch, Emmanuel, in your old age," she said, keeping her eyes straight ahead. "And it's not just your disease at work here. I'm beginning to think you've always been incapable of love."

"Righto!" he said, happy to have an antagonist at last. "Take it out on me now. Who was it that went along with this stupid idea of yours? Talk about selfish! You didn't consider at all what I've been through for the past few weeks, never mind what I've been through today. Did you expect me to enjoy myself there, stuck in the bathroom while the rest of you were having a fine old time discussing my infirmities? And don't tell me you didn't explain everything in excruciating detail. I could see it in their eyes, the way they inspected me when I came out, Winnie simpering, barely able to keep the tears from flowing, and old Abelard full of contempt for this sissy son-in-law his precious only daughter made the mistake of marrying."

"I think there's something wrong with your brain," said Emily.

That shut him up until they reached home.

"I'm taking a shower and going to bed," Emily said. Her stiff little walk, not looking his way.

Emmanuel, lying down on the couch to reflect, thoroughly ashamed of his behaviour. Why did those mean and nasty words come out of his mouth, despite his gentle and loving heart? For he did love them all: his wife and sons, his parents, Winnie and Abelard, his niece and nephew, his sister Amanda, though he drew the line at his brother-in-law. To his own embarrassment, he was often brought close to tears by the love he felt. It suffused his being. He loved his secretary Rose, his colleagues at work – most of them – the check-out girl he always went to in the supermarket, even if he had to wait in a longer line-up. He loved the starving little children in Africa displayed on TV. He loved Juhan Lipp and his daughter Anna Fedora. After all these years of being the faithful and devoted husband and the concerned and helpful father, how could she say that he was incapable of love?

30

IT was definite now. The verdict confirmed. His future decided.

"You can get dressed now," the technician said.

"Did they find anything?" Emmanuel asked.

"The results will be sent to your doctor. He'll call you after he reviews the report."

"It's my body," he complained. "It's my life."

"Sorry, sir. It's the rules."

Still shaky from being laid out flat for so long upon the narrow steel tablet, the whole length and breadth of him inserted into a metal tube like sausage meat in a casing, his vulnerable, unprotected body covered over with a sheet, his feet sticking out from under, his shoes, which they told him not to remove, needing a polish. Calm, he had to remain calm, though they indicated there was a buzzer near his right hand just in case he needed it.

"If, for any reason, you panic," the technician reassured him, in a tone indicating that this would be totally ridiculous.

Pleasant thoughts, they told him to think pleasant thoughts. At the lake when he was a boy. Peeing through his swim trunks, the water warming around his legs. At the tennis courts. His body dripping. In the evening, easing up his game to volley with Bonita. Her buttocks encased in khaki shorts, a moist stain spreading from the small of her back down her crack as she bent over to pick up the ball. Her breasts jiggling under her T-shirt as she ran. *Pew, you're all sweaty*, she said, wrinkling up her cute little nose when he kissed her. He was wet, there was no doubt about that. Feeling himself stirring. Wouldn't do to rise up under the sheet. Not in these present circumstances. Opened his eyes to check things out, but closed them again quickly. The top of the tube directly above his face, a thin row of lights like a zipper.

The humming of the machine suddenly stopped, followed by an interminably long period of silence. Perhaps there had been a power failure. An earthquake. An errant asteroid. A terrorist attack. They had forgotten him here in the tube, forever entombed. His fingers twitching toward the panic button. Then, at last, reverberating within his skull, a voice: WE HAVE TO REPEAT PART OF THE TEST. REMAIN PERFECTLY STILL.

They must have discovered the problem and wanted to double check. Engorged, inoperable, a tumour lodged firmly in his cerebrum. Definitely there was a pressure within the frontal lobes, indicating a lump twice the size of a golf ball pushing at his skull. They'll be sorry now. THEY'LL BE SORRY NOW. Who? Why? The answers escaped him. *Juhan, do you hear me? I'm dying too.* Pleasant thoughts, pleasant thoughts. Anna Fedora in white chiffon, her long pale hair unfurled, her blue eyes upon him, taking his hand and leading him upward. *Every human being must face the ultimate fate, Emmanuel, it's the price we pay for being alive.* Her precise and uncompromising diction, soothingly firm, promising order in the world.

THAT'S IT. YOU'RE ALL DONE.

A vision of himself, waddling away down a long narrow corridor, becoming smaller and smaller until he disappeared entirely. Done. DONE FOR.

An impatient honking of a horn brought him back to actuality. Stopped at a red light, now green.

"Yes. Yes. Yes," he muttered and pulled ahead at a snail's pace, remarking with perverse satisfaction that the light had turned red again and the car behind him was left waiting at the intersection. He turned in at the next parking lot, deciding to walk around a bit to clear his head. No sense in becoming a hapless victim of irrational road rage before his allotted time was up. Under a tortured sky, hands deep in the pockets of his coat, his body braced against the strong March wind, he shuffled down the avenue toward the public park where dogs were allowed to run free, chasing balls, retrieving sticks, sniffing the marvellous variety of smells the world had to offer, marking out new territory. A dog's life, short but always full of hope, despite being spayed or neutered, hunting instincts appeased by kibbled bits. Yippee, it's time for my walk, for my biscuit, for my supper. Unaware that soon it would all be over, the final trip to the vet.

Always viewing himself as a man who stood firmly on his own two feet, he had never prayed and he was not about to resort to asking for any extra help from above in this present extremity. But he wished, he wished with all his heart that he might live. Full of despair at the human condition, watching ancient dogs trail behind old men, surprised perhaps that they could no longer jump up a tree after a squirrel, that their joints pained in the morning, that it took them so much longer to do their duty in the backyard, but taking it all in stride, living in the present, unaware that soon it would be their turn to leave the external world with all its pains and pleasures, to unite again with the numberless horde of dead dogs and the countless puppies yet to be born.

"Here, pooch," Emmanuel called, holding out his hand. A golden retriever, a puppy, waggling his whole body with the joy of being, his tongue hanging halfway to his knees, allowing himself a brief scratch behind the ears before bounding off to his mistress, a young woman carrying a shiny red leash.

"Come on, Charlie," she called. "Sorry, sir, he's just a pup."

Oh, to be a pup again, with the whole world and all of its scents still before him. Yet what would he have done differently? Emily. He loved Emily. She was his rock, his anchor, his solace in the storm. And his boys? Even the thought of ever losing them rang alarm bells in his chest. Not to worry. Not to worry. It was true he hadn't accomplished much in life, but he still wanted to apprehend it. Desperately. A whole new millennium stretched out before him, full of joys and innovations and disasters. If he lived to be as old as Juhan, half of his life was yet to come. If he weren't dying now, he could possibly live to be a hundred. Life expectancy was increasing daily. His sons would be in their seventies, his grandchildren middle-aged. Individuals not yet conceived he might know and love. No, no, no, he did not want to give this up. He didn't want to die. Not now. Not yet. Maybe not ever.

Too agitated to sit any longer, Emmanuel got up to walk back to his car. Quite possibly this would be the last week, the final day of his life. No longer remembering his name, his address, how he came to be where he was, wandering the streets of the city in his filthy blue coat, a concerned passerby calling 911. *Lost, Officer, I'm lost. Name, address, telephone number? Don't know. Don't remember.* Searching through his wallet for identification. Calling his home number first, then his office. *Emmanuel Taggart you say? No, no one here by that name.* The gap of his absence already filled like a hole in a puddle.

31

THE day yawned before him as he headed home to his empty house. Emily was on March break, off by herself to visit Gerry. They had planned to take this trip together despite Emmanuel's unexpected illness, but then his MRI test was scheduled right in the middle of the week and they decided that this was more imperative than to see their son.

"Given your sentiments about 'family obligations,' it's just as well we can't go," Emily had opined, harbouring a grudge and biting her lip in disappointment.

"You should know me better by now than to pay attention to everything I say," Emmanuel defended himself.

He was sorry too. They hadn't seen Gerry since the previous summer and had never met Pam, his live-in girlfriend. "There's no reason why you shouldn't go, Em," he pointed out suddenly, an unselfish offer from the depths of his generous heart.

She hesitated, a worry pucker between her brows.

"I'll be all right, Em. Honestly," he assured her. "I'm a big boy now and these stupid tests, they're just routine, as you say. You go on and have a good time. You deserve it, with everything you've had to put up with lately."

He was quite pleased with this performance. A big grin upon the cockles of his heart. Yet he didn't really expect her to take him up on it.

Feeling a certain amount of guilt for thus deserting him – though, if truth be told, he had been more than impossible to live with lately – she spent the weekend cooking and baking a freezerful of Tupperware containers clearly labelled with the contents.

"All you have to do is stick it in the microwave," she instructed him. "And I expect you to eat while I'm away. You promise?"

"You can count on me," said Emmanuel, eager for her to get going now that the decision had been made. For a few days at least, he could do whatever he pleased without having to explain himself to anyone.

But now, after the test, he was restless. Afraid of the dark thoughts that kept reappearing in his mind. He wanted desperately to talk to somebody, a human touch. Someone to soothe his brow, to tell him it was all right. Emily had abandoned him. There was only one person he could think of, his recent vision of her still fresh in his consciousness. Anna Fedora, Juhan's daughter. She'd know what to say to calm him down. It was possible she might be in need of comfort as well. Lonely after the death of her father. He had been so full of his own despair, it was shameful how he had neglected her. Her back straight, rigid as ice – but also brittle, easily broken. All it would take was a little warmth to melt her completely. There was no doubt about it, they needed each other.

Thus rationalizing, he dialled her number and listened to her answering machine. Since it was March break, he hadn't really expected her to be there, but it gave him some satisfaction just to hear her recorded voice repeating the same familiar message. He got up finally to pour himself a stiff drink of Southern Comfort, settling in, watching the talk shows, getting up only to bring the bottle closer to where he lay.

The loud, persistent ringing of the telephone woke him.

"Hello?" he croaked.

"You sound terrible," said Emily. "Are you all right?"

"I was asleep. What time is it? Where are you?"

"I'm at Gerry's," she said, her voice excited, bright, chirpy. "Sorry to call so late, but we just got in. How did it go?"

"What's that?" he said, feeling guilty suddenly, as if he had something to hide.

"Did they tell you anything?"

It was only then that the entire ordeal came back to him. "The doctor is supposed to call," he said.

"So we wait."

"So we wait."

Gerry on the line then. Uncommonly jolly. "Everything will be A-OK, Pops, you'll see."

"Yes. Yes. I'm all right," he lied.

His head swollen, his tongue a furry mole searching for water in a vast and arid plateau. Piercing needles of pain stitched across his forehead from one temple to another. In the bathroom, he retched into the toilet bowl. With a cold wet washcloth on top of his head, he went back to the kitchen and drank several glasses of ice water. Then he threw up again before passing out on the sofa for another eight hours.

Looking in the mirror the next morning, he couldn't believe how much he had degenerated in hardly a month.

Red-eyed and slack-jawed, with a two-day growth of beard, his sparse hair greasy and sticking out at odd angles, his body pale and flaccid from the weight he had lost. Possibly some of this apparent decay was caused by the bottle he had emptied the night before, but there was no doubt about it: here stood a very sick man.

"I have heard the mermaids singing each to each. I do not think that they will sing to me," he recited, sighing from the deep caverns of his heart, another line he remembered from Introductory English. He didn't really understand those words then, but they seemed full of meaning now.

By afternoon he felt slightly better and took out a container of food labelled *Lover's Chicken xxoo*. Little m was a devoted wife, there was no doubt about that. Putting up with his moods, pampering his peeves, ministering to his illnesses. For better or worse until... He tried not to imagine the rest, those remaining after him living out their lives without his awareness. *Grampa died when he was still a young man, before you were born even,* Emily would tell their grandchildren. *A fine man. They broke the mould after they made him.*

Life was indeed a sad business. It was almost inconceivable that everything else would still be here long after he himself was reduced to a pile of ashes – even this Tupperware container, offered up at a yard sale when Emily moved into a small apartment in the city, passed on to another household, containing different leftovers prepared by unknown hands.

To keep himself strong, he piled a hefty portion of chicken on his plate, but could manage only a couple of mouthfuls before his stomach heaved. Sorry, Emily. It's good, but I've been bad. Brought up well, but rotted in middle age. Never bloomed at all. He scraped what was left on his plate back into the plastic container and set it in the refrigerator. Perhaps he'd try again later.

Definitely he should get out of the house. Perhaps take in a movie. A man alone, a pervert in the darkness of the back row. Women furtively glancing over, changing their seats to move farther away. The loneliness of a deserted stranger. He opened the liquor cabinet, but the thought of another shot of anything repelled him. A cold beer might bring him out of the doldrums. Checking out the bar fridge downstairs in the family room, musty now with disuse. Even the aura of the sprawling teenagers who had made their home here for so many years had evaporated. Three beers left over from years ago. Emmanuel took them upstairs, turned off the basement light. Goodbye to all that, so long to the good old days, sharing chips and pop with his sons, hollering at the TV. *YES! GO! GO! GO! Did you see that, Dad? What a play!* Weepy Emmanuel. Feeling sorry for himself. Full of the past, hating the present, with no future to look forward to.

Pacing the floor, looking up *brain tumour* on the World Wide Web. Definitely he had the symptoms: headache, nausea, confusion, disorientation, mood and personality changes. A shot of whiskey to calm his nerves. If he lived alone, would he become an alcoholic? Dirty clothes flung in a pile on the floor, dishes in the sink, an unmade bed, a filthy toilet bowl, his beard growing long, his teeth turning green, crouched on a street corner begging coins for a cup of coffee. Anything could happen unless he exercised what small control he still had over his life.

Calling Anna Fedora again. Still no answer. She was probably travelling too. Off on some tropical beach with some other teachers.

Reading the paper, lingering over the obituaries. Most of the deceased seemed to be in their seventies or eighties, though there were quite a few younger. Some in their late teens and early twenties, tragically, due to motor vehicle accidents. Many had passed away peacefully after long illnesses and courageous battles with cancer. Others had succumbed suddenly at work or at home. Heart attacks, most likely. Emmanuel gingerly touched his own. No sense agitating oneself needlessly. Every day people died. It was sad, but it made him feel less alone.

He spent the rest of the night, until the early hours of the morning, leafing through old photograph albums. A couple of smiley youngsters in wedding gear, both long-haired and skinny. Was that really them? A picture of his father a few years before he died. About the same age as himself, he looked like an old man to Emmanuel even now. A great shot of Abelard and Winnie years ago: Canadian Gothic, old Abe in his striped coveralls, Emily hugely pregnant. The boys as babies, as toddlers, their innocent eyes staring into the camera, bright with expectation, gawky in their basketball uniforms in junior high. Snaps of birthday parties, of trips to Florida, of summers at the cottage. His whole life passing before his eyes. They looked so happy, all of them. And they were. They truly were.

What had happened?

32

YOU can't be both here and now and there and then. But waiting at the airport for her flight to arrive, Emmanuel had let his mind wander, so for a fraction of a second he wasn't quite sure. Crowded amongst businessmen with briefcases, searching the concourse with anxious eyes, was that her? It was only when her face relaxed into a smile as she spotted him that he raised his hand in welcome. She did seem altered somehow; an experience not shared always results in a minute transformation of the other. Or maybe he just looked at her differently, realizing, perhaps for the first time, that though their spheres intersected, she moved in one all her own. As did everyone. All together, yet apart. The beauty and mystery of each individual life.

She didn't even smell the same and felt smaller in his arms than he remembered when he bent down to kiss her.

"For a moment I didn't even recognize you in that crowd," she said. "Sans moustache and so slim and trim." Then, looking him full in the face with narrowed eyes, her expression became serious. "No word yet? How to you feel?" she asked.

"Still kicking," he replied.

They said nothing more as they waited for her

luggage, standing in a circle with other silent witnesses, all staring with rapt attention at the conveyor belt making its lazy rounds with two battered suitcases no one seemed to want. But then a steady flow of baggage began to drop down and the crowd came alive, pushing aggressively forward.

"There's mine," Emily cried, shoving him ahead. "Get it."

In the privacy of their car well out on the highway, Emmanuel finally asked about her trip.

"So?" he said.

"They're fine. Pam's great. They both send their love. They'll probably come for a visit in the summer. We talked about it. We should get a cabin at the shore again for a week, M, like the old times. Maybe Mike can come too." Enthusiastic. Living a life different from his own. Not even travelling along the same orbit.

Then she was silent, her profile momentarily visible to him in the lights of an oncoming car, her eyes fixed firmly on the highway, her foot ready to hit the brake even though Emmanuel was driving. She had looked like a stranger to him when she emerged at the airport, part of the nameless horde, walking swiftly, toting an oversized handbag, a chubby little woman with blond puffy hair and the spastic movements of a squirrel. Somebody's grandmother, perhaps. Surely not the girl he remembered. The one in the photographs. How did this happen? And when? *You marry one and, if you wait long enough, she'll double,* that's what his father used to say.

"Did you eat?" she asked.

"Most of it," Emmanuel lied. Before heading for the airport, he had thrown out the remainder of the food she had prepared for him that was still in the freezer. It seemed a shame to waste it after all her work, but it would make her feel better to find it gone.

"So Gerry, he seemed okay?" he asked, after another long period of silence.

"On a higher plane than the rest of us, as usual," Emily said, employing an accent not familiar to him. "Pam is good with him, though. Takes him down a peg." But she didn't elaborate further.

Emmanuel left out, abandoned. She had become an intimate in a circle of intellectuals, presided over by their eldest son, of which he had no knowledge, in a place he had never been. And she was obviously not going to allow him entrance, hoarding secret knowledge she would someday use against him. He had been waiting for her to come home, but he was not pleased to see her. There were definite adjustments to be made. They drove the rest of the way in silence.

"Why don't you fix us a drink and I'll go unpack," she chirped when they got home. "I brought you something." Returning shortly with a ball cap bearing the name of Gerry's university that she stuck on his head.

Two old fools. The has-beens. Mom and Pop, sipping whiskey and sitting side by side on the sofa with nothing more to say to each other. Familiarity breeding strangers. So much stored up inside that could not be released. For awhile Emmanuel sat patiently waiting for his wife to explain herself, to reveal things he did not know, but finally he turned on the TV. She picked up the newspaper then and they made brief comments to one another once in awhile: "Did you read this, M? Unbelievable!" or "Watch this commercial, Em, haw haw." Back to normal, as if she had never been away.

The call came Sunday night.

"It's for you," Emily said, holding out the receiver with a penetrating look.

"Who is it?" Emmanuel mouthed silently.

Doctors didn't usually telephone on the weekend, no matter what the emergency. His heart pounding, his palms beginning to sweat. His life on the line. The final verdict. Sawing through the skull. *Pack up the slippers and robe, Emily,* just in case he survived the operation. His left hand supporting his heart, he reached for the receiver.

"This is Anna Fedora. I saw your number listed so many times on my answering machine, I thought it might be something urgent."

"Yes," he said. "Oh. yes," he repeated, desperately trying to think of something that would work both ends toward the middle. He could feel Emily's eyes boring into the back of his skull, her ears perked to pick up every nuance.

"Emmanuel Taggart? Do I have the right man here?"

"Yes, that's right," he said.

"Oh," she said. "I understand. You are presently in the act of dissembling in front of your wife." A smirk of amusement apparent in her voice.

"Yes," he said. "Look, I'll have to talk to Emily about this and call you back. When would be a good time? Would tomorrow be all right?"

"Tomorrow I have a meeting. How about Tuesday? Late afternoon."

"Great. Thanks. Hope to see you then."

Now to gather all his faculties, to bring forth every bit of skill developed throughout his long lying life in order to convince his wife she had nothing to fear from this appointment on Tuesday, that, in fact, it was to their mutual benefit, that, in fact, she should *urge* him to go. His head hot with confabulation. A deep sigh to let out an accumulation of steam. Heading for the bathroom to give himself more time.

"What is it?" Emily asked.

"I'll tell you in a minute," he said. "Nature calls."

It was imperative he tell the truth, twisting it only a quarter of a turn or so to give him the advantage. That's what had always worked in the past. The outright, outrageous lies, once found out, were the ones that could get one in trouble. It would be easy to say that someone from the office was calling, or a telemarketer, or just a woman taking a marketing survey – what a goddamn nuisance! – but there was no way of knowing if Emily had recognized the voice when she answered the phone, or whether Anna had perhaps even identified herself. Then he'd be done for. His goose cooked. His cookie crumbled. The upright image he had cultivated throughout the long decades of their marriage smashed to smithereens. No, he had to admit it was Anna who called to ask him about something. About the insurance? He had used that one already countless times and had disposed of it. For cocktails and dinner? Both Emily and himself. Mr. and Mrs. Taggart. As a gesture of appreciation for being so kind to her father. Relieved, he flushed the toilet and, in front of the mirror, prepared his face to dissemble.

33

EMILY sat waiting, her hands folded in her lap.

"It was Anna Fedora," he said. "The woman whose father just died? The old man whose car I hit? I went to visit him in hospital to let him know I was still alive? Heh, heh. You remember? Anyway, she's grateful, the daughter. Wants us both to come to dinner next weekend. As a gesture of appreciation for being so kind to her father. I said I'd talk it over with you and call her back."

"I know you're lying, Emmanuel," she said. "You're not a good liar."

"For godsakes, Emily. Whenever there's a woman involved, you go off the deep end." He raised his voice at her, insulted. "After almost twenty-five years of marriage one would think you'd have learned to trust me by now. Jealousy always was one of your deadly sins, Em, as I've said many times before. What are you thinking? The woman's inviting us both for dinner. Would she be doing that if there was anything going on? Besides, as I told you, she's older. About to retire."

"What does she look like?"

"Tall. White hair. I don't know. I never really looked at her. A mathematician," he emphasized heavily.

He was doing well. Emily hesitating now, not quite so sure of herself, chewing on her lower lip. "Do you want to go?" she inquired.

"Go where?" he said. "Oh, the dinner. I don't know. I mean, the woman is making an effort here, Emily. But, then again, maybe we shouldn't get involved. Avoid future commitments. It was enough to have to deal with the crazy old coot, her father. I'll just say, *Thank you very much but my wife has already made plans for next weekend.* That should put her off."

Cruel and disloyal. Cruel and disloyal. As he reached for the remote control, he noticed his wife's eyes were pink, tears quietly making their way down her cheeks.

"Emily, what is it?" he asked, alarmed.

"Emmanuel," she wailed, "how could you!"

"What?" he asked, genuinely puzzled. What had he done now? What had he said?

"I thought you'd been acting like this because you were sick, because you had terminal cancer or something, because you were frightened to death of whatever it is that's wrong with you. I never suspected it was because you were having an affair." Crying now in earnest, big sobs, snivelling.

"Who told you that?" he demanded. Ted and Lila? he almost sneered out loud, but bit his lip just in time. No sense giving out more information than was absolutely required in a case like this.

"No one. I just know. A wife can sense these things. You've been lying, Emmanuel. Covering up. It's this woman, Anna Fedora, isn't it? That's what it's been all along. When you said you got lost. When you said you were visiting at hospital. There was never an old man, was there? And to think how I've put up with your stupid moods and your constant whining and your childish outbursts of temper because I thought you might really be seriously ill. And how I've coddled you and tried to make you feel better, and held your hand and worried about you. And not only me. Your sons, too. Even my parents. How could you be so unbelievably selfish?" The tears stopped now. Red anger taking over. The sparks flying. Emily's little hands making fists, her knuckles white.

"It's not true. It's not true," Emmanuel stoutly defended himself.

"I realize it's not true. Now," she said. "All this play acting about going to the specialist. Did you actually have your body scanned when I was away? By a machine, that is. Or is all that a bloody lie as well? To think that a person I've devoted my life to for twenty-five years would stoop so low." She got up then and Emmanuel was afraid she was going to throw something at him. A jar of mustard pickles smack dab in the face, shattering his nose, ruining the upholstery. But Emily had always been more in control than he was.

"Call her. Call her right now and ask her if anything is going on. I'll dial her number myself if you want," he dared her, getting up also and walking to the phone. The risky strategy of a desperate man. He could see her hesitate, in a quandary, not so sure of herself anymore. "Go ahead, Emily, make a fool of yourself," he said, proffering the receiver, pretending to search for the number in the phone book. She watched him suspiciously, her lips pressed down like her mother's. His fingers pushing randomly at buttons. Come on, Emily, say something.

"No," she said. "Stop! This is our problem. We don't need to involve anyone else."

"According to your theory I've already involved someone else," he replied, hanging up, but retaining his threatening stance. "You stand there accusing a grief-stricken elderly woman who has just lost her father. Where's that compassion for the unfortunate, Emily, that you used to have in such copious amounts when you were younger? All you ever think about lately is yourself."

He shouldn't have said that last thing. He had gone too far. There was nothing left to do but to sink or swim. And he had always struggled to keep his head above water. "What were you doing for the past five days, for example?" Without pausing for an answer to interrupt the rhythm of his stroke, he continued. "Didn't you feel the least bit guilty about leaving me here to face all this alone? That MRI was no picnic, if you want to know the truth. It's not a patient-friendly machine. It was like spending time in a coffin, buried alive. And how do you think it feels to be waiting for a phone call day after day to confirm your worst fears? It's a wonder I *didn't* seek the comfort of someone else while you were away. But I didn't."

Almost to the shore now.

"And another thing. Give me some credit as a man, for godsakes, Emily. If I were to have an affair, wouldn't I pick someone *younger* than you?"

That ought to do it. He could see the data being digested in Emily's womanly brain. The attacks on her person in one column, the infirmities of her husband in the other. If the tears began to flow again, he had won.

"I'm sorry," she said calmly. "I must be tired from the trip. You're right, I shouldn't have gone away. Not with you in the state you're in. Tomorrow we'll hear something for sure. They inform a person as soon as possible when it's serious. Then we'll know."

34

RATHER enjoying his position of advantage in the matrimonial match, Emmanuel fumed with self-righteous indignation. How dare she accuse him, an upright representative of a rare breed, of an endangered species, a married man who had, for all these many years, actually been faithful to his wife? And not necessarily admired for it either. Even looked down upon in some circles, in fact. Considered prissy, like his father before him, a goody-goody tied firmly to the apron strings of the little woman. He had done it for her and she didn't appreciate any of it, giving him no credit whatsoever for the numerous temptations he had withstood, the opportunities passed by. Perhaps he ought to have succumbed just to show her. Asserting his manly prerogative. Since she already suspected him anyway.

If only she knew how much he had on his mind, literally, he thought, his fingers tentatively probing the furrows of his forehead, she'd be sorry. But he refused to be that cruel, even if she did provoke him past all endurance. There was no need to worry her unnecessarily before he knew for sure.

In the morning, however, he was somewhat ashamed of his assumed bravado the night before, for instead of kissing her own fingertip and pointing it in his direction as she normally did before leaving for work, she came right over to his side of the bed and placed her cool hand soothingly on his hot forehead. "You call me immediately when you hear something. If they say I'm not available, tell them it's an emergency. Promise?" She puckered her lips to pop a couple of smacks into the air above him and then she was gone.

He got up as soon as she left, and dressed, not daring to shower lest he miss the call. Hovering near the telephone, TV turned down low. At noon finally it rang, but it was only Emily.

"Nothing?"

"Nothing."

"Maybe you should get in touch with them," she suggested.

"If they don't have the common decency to let a patient know immediately what's wrong, the hell with them."

"Now there's a totally childish attitude. Do you want me to call?"

"Under no circumstances."

The next day, after again waiting all morning, Emmanuel did dial the number to check if the office was open. Hung up when the receptionist answered. *No news is good news*, his mother's voice reminded him. If the verdict was bad, he'd have to inform them in Florida, so his sudden death wouldn't come as too much of a shock. *Are you sure, son? That's what they tell me. I've got about a month, give or take.* But he wasn't going to sit around all afternoon to find out. They could leave a message. He had to see Anna Fedora. To talk about things he couldn't possibly reveal to his wife.

He abandoned his down-filled greatcoat in the closet and ventured out into the damp winds of late March protected only by sports jacket and jeans. No sense worrying about catching a chill. He had more important things on his mind. The dashing hero, displaying nerves of steel, his days numbered. Jeans hanging loose in the crotch but there was nothing he could do about that now. If he kept on losing weight, he'd have to buy a whole new wardrobe. Unless, of course, it became no longer necessary. They'd bury him in his old charcoal-grey suit, pinned in the back to make it fit. He must remind Emily he wanted to be cremated. Also he should make a living will, since it was more than likely his brain would depart before the rest of him followed. Perhaps it might be well on its way upon that final journey already, he thought ruefully.

It seemed such a long while since he had actually seen the living Anna, he found it hard to separate real conversations from those inflamed by his distressed libido. Strange, he thought, but even when intimacies happened only in dreams, one could no longer regard the other person involved in exactly the same way. Something special had occurred, whether she was aware of it or not. Ninety percent of all sexual experiences take place in the mind, he read somewhere, and he agreed one hundred percent.

"Hello there," she greeted him. "It truly is Man in the flesh! I was getting accustomed to your heavy breathing on the answering machine," she joked.

He shook her hand and then followed her into the kitchen where she poured out a measure of Jack Daniels for each of them.

"So?" she inquired, attending him with her bright blue eyes.

"They think I might have a brain tumour," Emmanuel blurted out. "I've been tested. There's nobody else I could tell." Not intending to say this much, but the words broke free before he got a grip on himself. The rims of his eyes beginning to sting. Quickly he gulped at his drink. "This hits the spot," he smacked, stretching his lips into what he hoped didn't resemble a vicious leer.

"That's not good," she commiserated. "Are they able to operate?"

"Not sure. Still waiting for the specifics."

"I'm truly sorry to hear this, Emmanuel."

They both sipped at their whiskey, contemplating the feeble position of man in the Universe.

"Some of us do have to leave the party earlier than others," she finally said, looking him straight in the eyes. "Good-byes are always difficult. Especially when you're not ready to go."

"Actually..." Emmanuel began. He was going to tell her the complete truth, that what he was waiting for, actually, were the results of the test, but it seemed to be an insignificant and minor detail merely since he had already convinced himself he was dying. "Actually, I'm ready to face whatever happens," he said, squaring his shoulders, firming up his chin, not able to meet her gaze, taking another big swallow of whiskey instead. "Getting my affairs in order. Seeing people I care about."

"*Mis on on*," she remarked. "One of my father's sayings: What is, is. It's your view of it that makes a difference. How is your wife handling this?"

Emily? He didn't want to think about Emily.

"She's been away. On vacation. I haven't told her yet."

He tried to keep his voice flat so he wouldn't sound

like he was peevishly whining. "She knows I had some sort of a test, but she thinks we're still waiting for the results. I figure it this way: why torture the woman before it's absolutely necessary. She'll find out soon enough."

A stab of guilt made him bite down on his tongue. But it wasn't really a lie. "That's why I wanted so badly to see you," he continued. "That's why I called you so many times. I had to tell someone, and I knew you would understand. I trust you, Anna, just like I trusted your father. Strange as it may seem, I feel like I've known you all my life."

Anna, appraising him from her blue eyes. She seemed to look right through his bumbling inaccuracies to perceive his soul. And accept it for what it was. Like Juhan had. He loved the tilt of her chin, the curve of her mouth, her reluctant dimples, her mass of white hair forming a halo around her face. He always had been partial to long hair. And yes, he had to admit it, the softness and strength of her body, which even now he wished to explore, getting hot with the thought, perspiring, a pressure in his genitals. He wasn't going to waste another moment with tittle-tattle. He wanted to know everything about her.

"Whatever happened to Asshole Fedora?" he asked bluntly.

"What!" she exclaimed, amused.

He hadn't meant to approach the topic quite that way, but the appellation had imprinted itself onto his brain.

"Sorry," he said. "Most men are at one time or another, or want to be," Emmanuel amplified, acutely aware of Emily's forefinger with the kiss still upon it pointing in his direction.

"He was irrational, true," Anna said, "but not in the way you're thinking. Fedora was nothing like most men. He was a mathematician. My professor, actually, in graduate school. He knew more about elliptic equations than anybody else in the world. But less than nothing about much else."

"Your father mentioned something like that."

"I thought he loved me, but he only loved his work. The worst thing you can do in life is to look for your own fulfillment in others, as I did. For five years he isolated himself in his study, hoping to discover a new theorem, a truth that would stand up to eternity. A worthwhile goal, I thought at the time, giving up your life to pursue an idea, and supported him as much as he would allow." She looked down at her hands, her ringless fingers.

Emmanuel didn't say anything, waiting for her to go on.

"Finally, it killed him."

"Metaphorically?" Emmanuel asked, using one of Emily's words.

"No. No. An actual bullet in the brain. I found him in his study one morning. He left a note: *I have lost confidence in my ability to arrive at a conclusion.*"

"That's awful!" Emmanuel said, shocked.

"Creating mathematics can be a painful and mysterious experience. He had no room in his life for anything else. He never should have married. And I never should have married him. I left the university then, and moved back here to be near my parents. My mother was sick and dying. I began teaching at the community college and have been there ever since."

"Do you like it? Teaching?"

"There have been moments, and, as my father always

said, it is the moment that matters. It's difficult – like you yourself pointed out, Emmanuel – to excite students about mathematics, yet it is the true language of Nature. Numbers are hidden in everything, from the harmonies of music to the orbits of planets. All else dies, languages change, scientific theories are discarded, but mathematical proofs last forever. The problem is that in order to be a creative mathematician, you have to master an immense vocabulary because everything in the world can be explained in terms of numbers. Most people can't be bothered. Yet mathematics describes the nature of the Universe and each breakthrough gives scientists a better vocabulary to explain the phenomena around us. I truly believed in what Fedora was trying to accomplish. Unfortunately, by killing himself, he destroyed both what was and what could have been."

Anna. Anna, Emmanuel was thinking, still searching for truths that were beyond the fallibility of human judgement. Yet there was a vulnerability about her that negated all absolutes.

"What I thought I wanted when I was very young," Anna continued, "was to be a real mathematician. One of the great ones. A woman in a man's world. My mother's early ambition coursing in my veins. But when I married Fedora I thought it would be sufficient to nurture his quest. Also, I wanted children. Things didn't work out either way."

"I'm so sorry, Anna," Emmanuel said. He wanted to take her hand, to touch her, but she was too far away. All alone in the world.

"*Mis on on*. In Estonian there is no future tense."

"Why is that?" Emmanuel asked.

"As a people we learned resignation. You can't always get what you want. But we're stubborn as well –

what must be done is done. And that's enough for today's lesson. I think you've been very patient, Emmanuel, especially for a man who always hated math. It helps sometimes to examine absolutes when you have to face the fact of being human. I'd offer you another" – she indicated his empty glass – "but I presume you have to drive back to Exit 13, Banbury, 125 Maple Street, fourth house on the left."

"I'd better get home. I left Emily a note saying I went for a drive and if I stay away too long she might start suspecting I got lost again." He smiled.

"It is not my place to advise other people what to do," Anna said, "but wouldn't it be easier if you told her the truth?"

At the door he put his arms around her and held her tightly against him. She didn't resist. But she didn't hug him back either.

"Anna. Anna," he whispered into her hair. "Thank you, Anna. I needed this."

She pushed him away gently and once again looked directly into his eyes. "I can see why my father took a liking to you. You're so...uncalculated. Take care of yourself, Emmanuel. Things might not turn out as badly as you think."

35

FULL of Anna as he drove through the dusk, traffic sparse on his side of the highway, the long line of cars travelling the other way, home from the city. She could be warm and accepting, yet so distant. Living in a world of numbers, of absolutes. An ache in his heart. For her. For himself. For all the people in the world longing for happiness, barking up the wrong tree. Everything Anna wanted in life had eluded her, yet she seemed to possess an inner strength, like Juhan. She had hoped for a family, children. Something he had taken completely for granted. Until his boys flew away, leaving the big cuckoo bird in an empty nest, with his little wife still fluttering around proffering choice tidbits from her devoted beak. Almost like strangers now, living lives increasingly unknown to him, their telephone conversations filled with meaningless idle chatter. Keeping in touch, but barely. Like with his own father. A man whose habits and irritations he remembered intimately, but whose essential being would remain a mystery forever.

Emily was preparing supper when he arrived home. "Hi hon," she greeted him. "Nothing yet, I guess?"

Emmanuel, his brain filled to the brim, was momentarily taken aback by the question, until he remembered. "Nope."

"That's just awful," she said. "Didn't they say they would call even if the test didn't show anything?"

"Yup."

"Why you don't call them? I don't understand."

"Nope."

Blowing steam out of her mouth, the exasperated wife of this exasperating man, not aware that knowing the facts would leave him with one of two intolerable alternatives: definitely doomed or incredibly foolish.

"Did you call that woman?"

"What woman?"

"The old man's daughter. To tell her we're not coming."

When you don't know what to say, it's best to keep your mouth firmly shut and Emmanuel did just that.

"The reason I'm asking," Emily continued, tired of waiting for a reply, "is that maybe we *should* go. The woman probably would appreciate some company right now if she was the main caregiver for her father all those years. That can be terribly hard on a person. While it's going on and when it's finally over." The old, generous-hearted Emily surging to the forefront, assured by her perfidious husband that the other woman posed no threat to her marital security. An older woman. A math teacher. How could she not sympathize?

But Emmanuel didn't want to share Anna with anyone, most particularly with his own wife. His time with her was too precious to be wasted in idle chitchat, sipping cocktails and nibbling peanuts, speaking predictable words heard hundreds of times before, telling the same old stories, repeating the same tired jokes, filling the room with meaningless patter that became louder and more raucous as more drinks were consumed. *I think everybody had fun*, Emily would say, cleaning up afterward, *but I'm glad it's over.*

"I called her already," said Emmanuel, "and told her we couldn't come."

"We'll make it another time then. Why don't we invite her here? Why don't I call?"

"No," Emmanuel said, but too emphatically.

"What is it, M?" she said, sitting down, her face tight, prepared for more than cursory chatter. "Let's be honest with each other. We owe our years together that much at least, don't you agree?"

"All right, Emily, you win." Emmanuel sighed and sat down heavily beside her. "I guess I haven't told you everything exactly as it happened. I didn't want to complicate our lives. I didn't want your imagination to run wild as it sometimes tends to do."

Emily, wringing her hands, her lips pressed downward, prepared for the worst.

"The truth is, that day I became sick and lost my way, I ended up in the house of a young woman."

"Anna Fedora?"

"No. No. Someone else. I don't even know her name."

"So you're not in love with her then?"

"What? Of course not. For godsakes, Em, stop trying to put your own interpretation on everything. You've read too many romantic novels in your life. They've perverted your outlook."

"It does happen, you know. Even when you least expect it."

"Well, this had nothing to do with love or romance

or even sex. I was sick as a dog. I got lost, as you know. Don't ask me how or why. I stopped at a house to ask directions. The woman who came to the door acted as though she had been waiting for me. She invited me in, the table was set, dinner was cooked. Before I could explain myself, she had me sitting down facing a plateful of lasagne. She had two little girls – cute – and a dog named Deal. After dinner, when she went upstairs to put the kids to bed, I sneaked out. That's it."

"That's it?"

His story did sound rather far-fetched, he had to admit.

"And how does Anna Fedora fit into this fairy tale?" she asked.

"I felt terrible afterwards, of course. I wanted to explain, to thank the woman for her hospitality, to apologize for so shamelessly running out on her, but I didn't have a clue where the hell I'd been. So I drove around trying to find her. Trying all the exits. Surely you can't blame me for that. Then I ran into John Lipp. The rest you know."

Emmanuel felt pure and clean, absolved. That was it. In a nutshell. Anna was right. It was best to reveal the facts. No one, not even a wife, had the right to know or judge what was going on in the private recesses of someone else's brain.

"So why the big secret?" asked Emily.

"I told you. You've always been the jealous type. I wanted to avoid a scene. I didn't think you'd believe me. You'd be harbouring suspicions. Besides, I was – I am – sick, in case you've forgotten. I had other things on my mind. Here, I'll show you."

He got up and went into the garage. Digging under

the front seat of the car where he had hidden it. "Proof!" he shouted triumphantly when he returned, holding aloft the yellow pad inside its black vinyl covers. "Evidence for the defence!"

After he showed her the meagre record of his search, Emily sat in silence for quite awhile, picking at her fingernails, chewing on her lower lip. He could sense mountainous swells still breaking under the wispy blond hair. When at last she spoke, it was almost in a whisper. "I'm sorry, Emmanuel. I had no right to doubt you. But like I said, we owe it to our marriage to be honest with each other. I have something to confess as well."

36

"**Y**OU have to admit, M, we haven't been communicating lately. Not in a real sense. Not for a long time."

So it was going to be one of those harangues: *How to Improve Your Marriage in Six Easy Lessons.* What women's magazine had she been reading lately? Emmanuel shifted his position on the sofa, bored already, but trying not to antagonize the little woman any further.

"Maybe not ever, really," she said sweetly, trying to prevent an argument despite the pugnacity of the words. "But at least we used to have fun together, you and I. In the early days. When the boys were small."

An album of remembrance passed across his features, a glimmer of sunshine on a cloudy day.

"I didn't mind staying at home then. I was content to take on the role of homemaker. I thought it was what we needed as a family. Everyone develops a persona, but when that is no longer viable, a reaction often ensues and there may be unpredictable consequences. After Gerry left, I began to feel abandoned, worthless. You and Mike had so much in common, you'd be going here and there, watching sports down in the rec room, joking around. It was you and him against me. I became the outsider, the drudge, the one who gave the orders, the one who spoiled your fun."

Emmanuel did recall winking at his son more than once during that time and whispering "Menopause!" Obviously she hadn't appreciated his sense of humour.

"My only function in life," she went on, "was to pick up after you and serve you meals for no pay and very little recognition. I felt miserable and unwanted, and neither of you, to be frank, gave a damn. You were too busy cheering on your team." She held up her finger as if to prevent him from speaking, although he had given no indication he was about to say anything, his eyes searching for the remote control.

"I had to get out of the rut and get out of the house to become my own person again." Her voice louder now, more strident, combative. "That's when I decided to upgrade and took those courses in the city. It gave me a purpose in life. I began to feel like a new woman. Rejuvenated." She tossed a phony smile in his direction and tried to take his hand, but he pulled it away.

"Get to the point, Emily," he intoned, his teeth pressed patiently together, his lips barely moving. She was leading him somewhere he had no wish to go.

"Neither of us is anything special, M. I know that. But what we shared together is special. Our children, our memories. We have reached the age where our past has more authority than our future. The scales have tipped the other way. The future no longer stretches ahead of us like a bright, empty expanse but is closed in and overpowered by the past. There are only a few narrow paths left for us to follow. We can make some changes, sure, but we can never start all over again. Everything we've done thus far is the baggage we carry with us."

Choosing her words with care, picking at her fingernails to even off the cuticles. He felt like slapping her hands to make her stop fidgeting. Had she been snooping around in his brain? He had to admit that the idea had insinuated itself lately. Leaving his old life hanging in the closet beside his down-filled winter coat, while he took himself to a beach in Waikiki. Lying on a blanket with Anna Fedora.

"It was a while ago," Emily was saying. "And you have to keep in mind the important thing: I chose *our* life. I decided to stay. One can't ever find salvation in somebody else; it has to come from within. I began to realize that the breakup of a marriage is the same as a death. You can never again share those special memories with anyone else in the world: the birth of our sons, watching them grow. And they can never be replaced, those moments when a word, a look, a name is enough to bring back a whole lifetime of images. That's why I've been working so hard to make our marriage work. We have children together. We've shared the major portion of our lives. We've forged a bond. We'll always be together in a realm far greater than the physical. Our sons might be grown up, beginning lives of their own, but family continues. Wives, grandchildren – people yet unknown who will be connected to us intimately forever. And we should be there to welcome them, you and I." Her eyes watery with emotion.

Emmanuel felt himself turning into stone. Starting at the top of his head, his cheeks suddenly heavy, hanging downward like the jowls of a bloodhound, the pressure spreading into his chest, lodging in his intestines, his legs and feet numb. What was she saying? What did she mean? Emily?

"I'm only telling you this because I think we should be totally honest with each other. Especially now. In order to save what we have. In order to make it better. And I want you to remember that I chose to be with *you*, M. Twice."

She put her finger into her mouth and nibbled.

"Go on," he said, listening with both ears now, sitting forward, his bristles raised, his teeth on edge.

"After class we'd go out to get a cup of coffee or something and discuss the projects we were working on and such."

"We, we, we," Emmanuel cried. "Who is WE? I've been interacting with you for the past twenty-five years under the mistaken impression that *we* were WE."

"His name doesn't matter. I am not going to reveal it, even to you. He's a minister."

"Ha-ha-ha," Emmanuel laughed. "A sanctimonious affair."

"He's a nice man, truly, Emmanuel, a moral man. That's the reason I was attracted to him in the first place. He had such compassion, such insight."

"Did you do it?"

"Don't be crude," she said, looking at him full in the face for the first time since she began her confession.

"Who me?" Emmanuel said, pointing to himself. "God forbid I should say something like that in the spiritual presence of this sainted man."

"It just happened is all. We became friends. We talked about *everything*. He was so supportive. He gave me confidence as a person. And as a woman. He made me feel important, desirable even. And then one day we had to stay overnight in the city because of a snowstorm."

There was a long pause as both of them reviewed the

ensuing scene, the Big M breathing heavily through his nose, the little m sitting beside him with clasped hands and bowed head.

"Nothing came of it. It was over almost as soon as it began. He was married with young children. He had his reputation to consider. I never saw him again after the course ended."

Seriously wounded, the Big M. Not shot through the heart directly, but definitely hit hard in the ego. "Were you *in love* with this minister?" he asked, mincing the words, cutting them down to size with the sharp edge of his sarcasm.

"I thought I was at the time. Otherwise I never would have done what I did. You should know me well enough by now to realize that."

"I believed I did, Emily, I honestly believed that I did. But it appears now that I was wrong. And how about me? Do you *love* me? Or was your return to the bosom of your family prompted by the fact that the hypocritical bastard didn't want you for anything else except a little fun on the side?"

There was a slight hesitation before she answered, which did not go unnoticed by Emmanuel.

"To be completely honest, I *did* consider leaving, yes, not because of him but because of us. As I told you. But I decided to stay. I realized that what we had together was more important than anything else. That counts for something, doesn't it? You must admit it hasn't always been easy." She smiled at him, sniffling back tears, and tried to take his hand again.

"Apparently it wasn't as important as a hot night in some sleazy hotel," he hissed, the numbness he felt at the first shock of her deception giving way to red prickles of anger. He wanted badly to slap her hard across her simpering stupid face. Walked across the room to remove himself from the temptation. Slammed his fist into the wall instead, leaving a dent in the plaster and hurting his hand in the process.

"Honestly, I never thought you had it in you, Emily. You always were a bit of a goody-goody. Now I find out that all this time you've been falsifying yourself, pretending, conniving, lying outright, using your sleazy, scummy womanly wiles to make *me* feel guilty, accusing me of this and that, pretending to be jealous when I made the slightest reference to another woman, all the while covering up your own infidelities. I can hardly believe this! You are not the girl I married."

His mouth dry from all that sputtering, he poured himself a large glass of whiskey.

"No, I'm not," she was saying, "and it's about time you acknowledged that fact."

"Next you'll be telling me that this is my fault, along with everything else."

"There's a bit of truth in that, you know, Emmanuel, whether you want to admit it or not."

37

GRABBING his coat then, from out of the closet. Slamming the door. Revving up the motor of his car in the garage. *Varroom. Varroom.* Toxic fumes filling the enclosed space. Squealing the tires as he turned out of the driveway. He'd show her. How could she do this to him? He saw her again as she was when they first met. Her little hand in his. She fit so neatly under his arm. He felt strong and virile then. He promised to take care of her forever. Emily, oh Emily, what have you done, where have you gone?

Driving to the highway, automatically heading toward the city like he had every day of the week for all those many years. Putting in his hours at a meaningless job so he could support his family. Wasting his life. Aimlessly wandering, driven out of his own house. No longer Lord of the Manor. A cuckold. A goddamn cuckold. He should make a U-turn, drive over to see Anna, no excuses needed. But he refused to become one of those men who complained about his wife to gain the sympathies of another woman. He didn't want her to be the one attempting to put together the pieces of his ruined marriage.

And what would his loving spouse be doing now? Downing a glass of whiskey herself before calling her mother to tell her the good news. *He's left me, Mom. Dead? No, not yet. You'll be okay, hon. He never was much good you know, like Abelard always said. Better luck next time.*

Maybe he should get a hold of the man himself, the minister, causing cold sweat to break out upon the sanctified forehead, fear moistening the holy armpits, the wife and children in the next room cowering as he broke, if not his neck, then at least his little bubble. He should have insisted she reveal his name. Maybe he could find out at the university. E. M. Taggart, private investigator, seeking information at the registrar's office. *We're looking for a sexual predator, ma'am, enrolled in one of your classes a few years ago. A Reverend. May I see your registration records?*

He pulled into the empty parking lot by the office, but decided it might look suspicious if he stayed there. Cupped his hands over his mouth to smell his breath. Definitely alcoholic, though he felt absolutely sober. Still it wouldn't be good to be accosted by a cop, breathalyzed, made to count backwards from one hundred, made to walk the line, to touch his finger to his nose with his eyes closed. *I'm not drunk, Officer, I've got a brain tumour, honest.*

Back out on the street, driving south. It was obvious what he should do now. He had seen enough bad movies on TV to know how a typical twentieth century North American male was expected to assuage his anger and reassert his damaged masculinity in a situation like this. He should head for the nearest bar, get drunk and obnoxious, perhaps weepy, fall victim to some sleazy whore, and wake up the next morning in a dingy hotel room with a pounding hangover, the woman and his wallet nowhere in sight. That's what happened to men like him.

Breath stinking of whiskey, he drove aimlessly along the side streets of the city, where there was less likelihood of being apprehended as a drunk. Most people here were home now, relaxing with their families, the greenish glow of TV screens flickering from uncurtained windows.

When they first married, they lived in this sort of neighbourhood: large Victorian mansions converted into affordable apartments, close enough to the commercial centre of the city so they could walk everywhere. Hand in hand through the Public Gardens, stopping to admire flowers and feed ducks. Meeting for lunch in the deli across the street from where Emily worked. Selecting names for the baby. Gerald for a boy, they finally decided, Magrita for a girl. After Mike was born, Emily had her tubes tied, Magrita, never conceived, her DNA forever unrealized in eternal space.

"Magrita," Emmanuel whispered aloud, his vision momentarily blurred by a watery influx, high tide.

They had been happy then. In slow motion. Making plans for a future that seemed so special because it was theirs. Buying a house in the suburbs, heavily mortgaged. Checking out the schools. A good place to bring up kids, Banbury. The boys growing up before his eyes then, a speeded-up version, fast-forward, all of them happily smiling, waving bye-bye.

She had betrayed them. She had destroyed their conception of reality. His, and the boys' also, if they only knew. She had negated everything they believed to be true. His Emily. He curled down the corner of his lip at the irony of those words. She had never been what he had imagined her to be. He would never forgive her for that.

Pulling over to the curb, he rested his damaged brain on the steering wheel. How could she do this to him? To endanger everything they had together for a momentary thrill, so she would feel – what did she call it? – rejuvenated? Anger foaming to the surface, spilling over the edge. He was the man. He was supposed to have the precedent. It was expected of him. Emily herself had expected it. Accused him, even. Men who didn't have at least one dangerous liaison during the duration of a long marriage were considered suspect, not quite virile enough, pussy-whipped. One or two affairs, a few one-night stands that the little woman didn't know about, a tearful promise to reform when she found out, and the marriage would be better for it. Or so popular opinion would have it. What she had done to him was definitely a blow below the belt. A direct hit to his masculine ego.

His outrage gave him sufficient energy to raise his head and look around. Where was he anyway? Lost again? Here the buildings were newer and shabbier. Apartment duplexes. Rose, his secretary, lived in this section of town, 171 Washington, if he remembered correctly. Creeping slowly around the blocks, gawking at street signs. Rose had always been more than willing to commiserate. *O Lordy, Mr. Taggart, isn't that a goldarn shame*. Shaking her head, bright red lips puckered in dismay.

Parked in front of the house, he reconsidered. Maybe an unexpected visit wasn't such a good idea. At least he should have called first. Rose, nervously clearing up the refuse of her evening, gathering up bottles of nail polish and soggy pink wads of cotton, apologizing for the dirty dishes piled up on the counter by the sink, swiping her hand across her backside as she excused herself to go to the bathroom to smear her mouth with lipstick, to fluff up her thin hair. *O, Mr. Taggart, I wasn't expecting company.*

But it was too late now to change his mind, for a young boy in a black leather jacket came bounding down the steps, staring hard as he passed by. Emmanuel recognized him from the pictures she had displayed, Rose's son Rauncy, Rowdy, something weird like that. *Hey, Ma, there's a strange car parked out in front with a man sitting inside, staring in our windows. Are you in trouble, Ma? Are you being stalked?* Wouldn't want to cause Rose any more anxiety than she already bore upon her bony shoulders. Circumstances always seemed to conspire against him. Reluctantly he forced himself to leave the comfort of his car to walk up her sidewalk, open the heavy front door and press her buzzer.

38

"**L**ORDY, Mr. Taggart," she exclaimed when she opened the door. "Is that you?"

She looked different without her office get-up, in jeans and a sweatshirt, no make-up, her hair askew. Younger. Like a little girl living a hard life.

"I was just..." she said, fluffing up her hair with her fingers. "Please come in."

"I was just passing by and thought I'd drop in to see how everything was going," Emmanuel explained, assuming the more elevated tone he always used in his professional capacity at the office, chin lifted, eyes directed slightly downward, looking down his nose, actually, past Rose, into the cluttered apartment, where a teenaged girl lay sprawled on the rug in front of the TV with books and papers strewn around her. Rose's other offspring. Alana? Alicia?

"You've lost some weight, Mr. Taggart," said Rose, taking his coat. "My. My. You're looking good in spite of everything. Amelia, dear, you'll have to clear out and work in your own room. We have company. Mr. Taggart is here. From the office."

Amelia snorted and glared at him briefly, but then did as her mother told her.

"What can I get you? I have some sherry. I think maybe beer. Pop? Coffee or tea?" Rose moving around the small room, straightening pillows, wiping her hand across the coffee table, turning off the TV, fluffing up her hair again.

"A beer if you've got it, Rose. I don't want to be any trouble."

"No trouble. No trouble. Not to worry."

When she returned with two beers, she had applied lipstick, combed her hair, looked more like the Rose he remembered.

"Whew," she said.

"So how's everything going, Rose. At work, I mean. And for you personally too, of course."

"Fine. Fine. As fine as can be expected, that is. They've got someone now in your office. Part-time. Filling in. As you've been out sick for so long. A woman. A girl, actually, we call her, just graduated university." Her painted nails raked down her face to clutch at her cheeks, then folded under her chin as she pursed out her lips, nervous, wondering how he would react to this new bit of information. "When are you coming back, Mr. Taggart? We've all been wondering."

"Still waiting for the test results."

They replaced him with a woman! Not even a woman, *a part-time girl!* His whole life failing him all at once.

"Oh, Rose," he said, lowering his chin, downloading his tone, placing his forehead into his hand.

"Oh, Mr. Taggart," she said, her enormous brown eyes brimming over with sympathy.

For some time now he had been counting on the fact that there was indeed something physically wrong with him, something that would slice him out of the picture. A debilitating condition. A terminal disease which would put the remains of his life permanently into the hands of competent professionals. All he had to do was to think pleasant thoughts and they would take care of the rest. He could leave with a bit of dignity then. *Poor Emmanuel, after a long and courageous battle, and so young too.* But if it turned out to be nothing, then what! Incontestable proof of his total and complete inadequacy for all to see. A faker, a hypochondriac, a cuckold, of no use any longer to anyone. Discarded. Thrown out with the trash.

"Are you okay, Mr. Taggart?"

"Things haven't been going my way lately, Rose."

"Ain't that the truth," she sighed.

Silently sipping beer then, both preoccupied with their own cartload of troubles.

"You, Mr. Taggart, are a rare one. Not like some of the guys in the office I could mention, but won't." Her eyes flashing to the ceiling, blowing up air to cool off a hot forehead. "What I mean is, you're a real family man, not looking to fool around like a lotta fellas. My ex, for instance."

Emmanuel was not sure how to respond. Was Rose immunizing herself against what she might presume to be the purpose of this unexpected visit? Or was she longing for someone to talk to as well. Two wounded people hungering for sympathy. He thought it wiser to pursue the last option. "You've been divorced quite a number of years now, as I remember," he ventured.

"Nope. Still not divorced. Can't afford it. Bill took off when the kids were little. And on my salary? It's a good thing my parents help out or we'd be in the poorhouse." She laughed. A nervous titter, a protective covering for the bruises beneath, there being nothing funny in what she was saying.

"Bill, he liked the women. Wanted what he called an open marriage. He needed his freedom, he said. Once he even took me to a club for swingers. Royce was just a baby then. I thought he was treating me to a weekend out. Like a second honeymoon? Just goes to show how stupid I was. I spent the whole night in the bathroom, crying. It's been hard on the kids growing up without a father. Especially Royce. He's full of anger."

Rose, not used to performing a public recitation of her life, fiddling with her hair, pulling at her chin, stopping between each sentence as if reading a cue card.

"But as I say, *you*, Mr. Taggart, are one of the rare ones. A family man. They don't make them like that anymore."

"They broke the mould, Rose."

There was such an expression of sorrow on his face, that she raised her eyebrows and puffed out her lips. "I'm so sorry," she said. "Here I am talking about my own insignificant little troubles, when you must be…? With your illness and all. We miss you at the office, Mr. Taggart. You always cheered everyone up."

They had another beer then, with Rose continuing to do most of the talking, nervously filling the silence, Emmanuel providing the *oh yeses*, the *I know what you means*, further revelations about her unfortunate marriage, her unexpected offspring she had no idea how to control, especially now they were teenagers. *Oh don't get me wrong, Mr. Taggart*, she loved them both with all her heart and did, indeed, wish to devote the rest of her life to them, which wasn't, apparently, enough, given their attitude. They seemed to despise her in fact, or, maybe not her, actually, but everything she stood for. What they needed was a father to look up to, to give them the whatfor when they misbehaved. They blamed her for that too, she was sure, although they had never said it right to her face: if she had been more of a woman, she would have kept her man.

Rose, Rose, it's not true, he wanted to tell her, all teenagers are like that; but perhaps it was true. How did he know, the insides of everyone being so different from their outer shells, what they appeared to be quite the opposite, sometimes, of what they really were? Emily, for instance. He looked at his watch. It was nearing midnight. Sitting forward on the sofa, he intended to take his leave with some parting words of encouragement – Rose, unlike himself, had to be at work in the morning – when the telephone rang. One look at her face after her initial cheery hello told him it was too late to make his escape. Whatever had brought the hand not holding the receiver to press against her heart would keep him there as well.

"It's Royce!" she cried. "He's in hospital. In the Emergency Room. That was the police. They want me to come right away." Fingers fluffing through the hair. Grabbing both their coats from the closet. Shouting to her daughter. "Something's happened to Royce. I'll call you." Rushing out the door, down the stairs. "Do you mind, Mr. Taggart, driving me?"

Squealing the tires, speeding through dark empty streets, slowing at red lights for a look, but passing right through. *An emergency, Officer, we've got to get this woman to hospital.* An adrenalin rush, a sense of masculine power. *I'll take care of it, lady, I'll get us there even if it means a traffic ticket.* Dropping Rose off at Emergency before parking the car in the Visitors' Lot. Not crowded like the last time he was here to see Juhan. Years ago. His heart pumping dangerously close to the surface, he felt like crossing himself, knocking on wood, spitting over his right shoulder three times, anything, to propitiate the forces of evil. Running up the steps to the Main Entrance, two at a time, into the dusky interior. Everything eerily silent. A red arrow pointing to Emergency.

How many times had he imagined this, feared it, lying in bed watchfully alert after midnight, anticipating the scream of the telephone, until the welcome sound of the garage door, the son late, but safely home, trying to sneak past their anger into the shelter of his own bedroom.

"Royce Petrelli?" Emmanuel inquired at the desk, Rose nowhere in sight.

"2A. You can go right in."

In a small enclosure Rose was weeping beside a boy Emmanuel assumed to be Royce – although he looked nothing like the lad in the photograph he remembered – who was lying on the examination table fully clothed except for his leather jacket. No more than a child, really, this boy, with red miserable eyes in a pale and sullen face.

"Who's this?" Royce asked. "He don't look like no doctor."

"It's Mr. Taggart, dear. My boss from the office?" Reaching for a limp hand, stroking it, but the boy pulled it away.

"He took something," Rose explained. "The cops brought him in. They pumped out his stomach. He won't talk to me."

"Fuck," Royce mumbled.

They sat in silence for what seemed like interminable

hours until the doctor came in.

"Mr. Petrelli?" he said, nodding at Emmanuel. "It seems your boy got himself into some trouble here. Ingested a substantial amount of alcohol in a short time. We pumped out his stomach just in case he had taken something else as well. He's still drunk, but should be okay. Get him home to bed. Get him some counselling. The boy suffers from low self-esteem. Spend some quality time with him. Take him out to a ball game."

Emmanuel had opened his mouth to clarify the family situation, but the doctor was already gone.

Despite his sullen demeanour, Royce was surprisingly compliant when Rose put his jacket around his shoulders and they helped him out to the car. Perhaps the doctor was right – the boy's rage was directed inward and had not yet exploded into the world at large.

"I'm sorry, Mom," he was saying, and crying then, both of them sobbing together in the back seat.

"Don't worry, Rose," Emmanuel tried to comfort her as he deposited them on their doorstep. "You're doing the best you can and those kids will realize that sooner or later."

"Thank you, Mr. Taggart," she said, giving him a quick peck on the cheek. "You're wonderful."

He waited until the two figures, bent over to help each other up the stairs, made it safely inside the door before pulling away.

His secretary Rose, having to cope, coping, blaming herself for all the ugliness in her world. He felt the pain of his own unshed tears, a pressure in his sinuses, slapped the steering wheel hard with his gloved hand, but a warm glow had formed itself around his heart as well, a small flicker of his own worth emerging from the sewage field of his life. *Mr. Taggart, you're wonderful.* You made the effort. You did the best you could. You made sure you took your boys to the ball game and to McDonald's afterward. A boy like Royce should have a father. What was wrong with these men who abandoned their children when they needed them, searching the world for love that they left so carelessly behind? His sinuses paining again, feeling a deep sorrow for all the fatherless children everywhere.

39

THE dashboard clock showed 4:30. Hopefully Rose would take the day off, spend some quality time talking things over with Royce, who certainly was in no condition to get up and go to school in the morning.

Emmanuel was already driving through the outskirts of the city, heading home, before he remembered his own state of affairs and the warmth around his heart quickly cooled to ashes. Emily. For the greater part of his life she had been there for him, like a comfortable pair of old slippers he would automatically shove his feet into, always in the same place under his bed where he had left them the night before. How could she have done this to him? Even now he found the immensity of her deception difficult to believe. Or maybe it was his own gullibility that was harder to swallow. Emily, with her dyed puffy hair and pudgy armpits, embroiled in a love affair. And jolly old Emmanuel in the meanwhile, sharing quality time with their younger son, cheering on the team, eating popcorn in the family room. It seemed ridiculous, almost. Something that happened to other people. Something to laugh about together.

The night had turned damp and foggy as Emmanuel drove slowly through the empty streets, his eyelids beginning to feel heavy. Peering through the mist, he saw an oasis of light, a brilliant glow emanating from the darkness, a sparkling aluminum construction flashing huge red neon letters: EAT. Perhaps that wouldn't be such a bad idea, he thought. A coffee might wake him up sufficiently so he wouldn't become a hazard on the highway.

He felt quite at home sitting at the counter among all these men who had lost their sharp edges in the darkness: the habitual drunks looking for someplace still open when the bars closed; shift workers slowing down before heading home to sleep; truck drivers stopping in for an early breakfast, trading quips with the motherly waitress. They were welcome to loiter here before the city awoke and morning people, grouchy and harried, rushed in for a quick caffeine fix before heading to the job.

He ordered a full breakfast of scrambled eggs, hash browns, bacon, and toast, watching the short-order cook, a black man with the hands of a virtuoso, perform his magic. The grill his instrument, the long row of orders tacked up above him, his score, he flipped hamburgers, turned hash browns, cracked eggs, buttered toast, and filled the warmed plates with incredible speed. Emmanuel couldn't recall ever enjoying a meal as much. Wiped his plate clean with a piece of toast. Washed it all down with several cups of strong coffee. Joked with the waitress as he remembered his father doing: "Don't get this kind of treatment from the wife, young lady, would you consider coming home with me?" Grinned broadly to share the witticism with the cadaverous fellow sitting on the stool next to him, whose long stringy hair hung down over his turned-up collar and who had been nursing a cup of coffee and smoking home-rolled cigarettes.

"Norm here," the man said, holding out his hand and displaying a full set of brown teeth.

"Have one on me, Norm," Emmanuel said, sliding over a tenner, leaving another for the waitress. The generous-hearted Mr. Taggart on the town. Feeling the warmth of his largesse spreading through his veins, his tummy comfortably full, his head spastic with coffee, he smiled at the assemblage and waved to the cook who was too busy to notice, as he settled himself back into his blue greatcoat. He hated to leave, but he couldn't stay here forever.

It was already light outside. Emily was probably getting up now to discover his side of the bed still empty, his pillow plump, his sheet unrumpled. A worried little frown between her eyebrows, no one to kiss her forefinger to before she headed off to work. The highway empty on his side, the long line of commuters heading for their jobs in the city. When he arrived home, he was surprised to see her car still in the garage.

Then her familiar face filled with concern as she met him at the door. "Are you all right?" she asked.

He realized then how good it was to see her there waiting for him. So preoccupied with his own life and death, he had never even considered what would happen to him if she were the one to go. A surge of overwhelming love clutched at his heart, an almost unbearable pain, leaving his legs weak and rubbery. She had stood by him despite his indifference, his obstinacy, his glib assumption of his own superiority, his downright infantile behaviour. She was still standing by him now.

"I'll survive," he said dismissively.

"I'm glad to see you back safe and sound," she said, searching his face as she took his coat and then his arm to guide him to the sofa in the living room.

"I was really scared, you know, Emmanuel," she continued. "What you did was no joke. Not in your present condition. I spent practically the whole night on the telephone trying to find you, calling hospitals, calling the police. Of course they can't do anything. Not for forty-eight hours if the person missing is over sixteen."

"Wasn't that a bit extreme, Em?" he suggested. "Broadcasting my night out all over creation. What did you expect? After your…confession."

"You've been sick, M. You've been behaving strangely of late, you must admit. I thought you tore out of here to cool down, that you'd be back. When it got to be after midnight and you still weren't home, I was imagining all sorts of horrible things. I called everyone I could think of, trying to find you. Some of your cronies from work. Your secretary, Rose, but she was out, her daughter said. Finally I thought of Anna. I'm sure I woke her, but she was really nice about it."

"You called Anna? My Anna? Anna Fedora?" A flash of heat down the backbone. Face beginning to boil.

"What other Annas do you know? It was when she informed me about your brain tumour that I went over the edge. 'Didn't he tell you?' she says. 'About the test results?' she says. 'It's not really my place to give out the information,' she says, 'but under the circumstances…' Which I now know was all a lie, by the way," her voice betraying her growing irritation. "But last night it really got to me. I was acting under the mistaken impression that they had indeed discovered a tumour in your brain. That you hadn't told me because you didn't want me to worry. That's when I started calling hospitals."

"I'm sorry, Em," Emmanuel said and meant it, his

humiliation like a bucket of cold water, drowning any remaining vestiges of resentment.

"This morning I finally took it upon myself to call the doctor's office. There's nothing wrong with you, Emmanuel. It's all in your head. His secretary told me. She was surprised you weren't informed, but she had been sick with the flu, she said, so there must have been some sort of a mix-up. THERE IS NOTHING WRONG WITH YOU!" Emily shouted. "You're A-OK from top to bottom. They have examined every inch of you and you're a perfect specimen physically. You've been going to the wrong sort of specialist. Do you understand what I'm saying?"

Emmanuel said nothing. He had made a total ass of himself. Nothing wrong? What was the matter with him then?

"Or were you just pretending they didn't tell you? To get some special attention and sympathy?"

"That's a bit of a blow beneath the belt, Emily. How could you say that to me?" Insulted to be accused of lying when he had been telling the truth.

"I thought I knew you, M," she sighed, "but what I know about you only skims the surface. You contain hidden shallows I never even suspected existed."

I'm not as shallow as you think, he wanted to defend himself. *I never was. I was just content to skim over the surface. I never took time to examine the depths. I'm ready now, Emily, you've got to believe me.* But he couldn't say it, not yet; the waters were still too turbulent.

"When I think of how worried we've all been. Myself, the boys, my parents, while you…" She snorted in disgust. "We'll have to call them right away. Tell them the good news that it's been in your head all along. And I am not referring to some sort of imaginary brain tumour."

"Now look here, Emily." Emmanuel began to repair what was left of his tattered image. "Have you considered at all what it is like to wait for the verdict? Not to know whether you're going to live or die. The specialist mentioned a tumour. I didn't want to say anything about his diagnosis until they knew for sure. They never did call me to tell me what was what."

"The fact remains, Emmanuel, you *wanted* something to be wrong with you. You were hoping for a tumour. Admit it."

"I don't have to listen to this."

But he had abdicated whatever advantage he may have had by being found out.

"We're not engaged in some sort of a ball game here, Emmanuel. I'm not your adversary, nor your little m any longer, for that matter, cheering you on. We're grown up people here, human beings in the same boat, trying to live out our lives the best way we can. I will throw you a life preserver, but I refuse to be your slop bucket."

Emily going to the kitchen then to heat up a can of soup for lunch, answering the telephone, her eyes upon him, evaluating.

"Yes, yes, he's home. He's fine. There is no tumour, we found out today. The tests came back negative. No, no. Thank you for calling. I'm sorry to have bothered you so late last night. Yes, ha ha. I need it."

"Anna Fedora," she said, hanging up.

"Emily," he said, "you're like a disease. You spread yourself everywhere. You infect every portion of my life."

"Heat up your own goddamn soup then," she said. "I'm going to bed."

40

EMMANUEL dreamt of someone approaching him silently from behind, placing both hands gently upon his shoulders. *There is nothing wrong with you*, a voice said. Quickly he turned, half-expecting to see Juhan, but his own face was looking at him with love and acceptance. A deep peace descended upon him. He opened his eyes, his heart filled with joy. He was not going to die. Not yet. He had been allowed more time. To repair any damage he may have done, to give a helping hand, to apprehend, to enjoy, to create, perhaps even to gain some wisdom before he had to face death again.

You're like a child, Emmanuel, Emily had told him. *You expect life to reward your good intentions. Don't you know yet that life is indifferent. You have to find your own rewards.*

There was a formidable task yet ahead of him: he had to reconnect himself to the outside world, not as a person who was dying, a man seeking commiseration or pity, but as someone who was not afraid of accepting existence once again with the full knowledge that all love is lost in the end, for death separates everyone. He must also gather up the dregs of his personal integrity, drive to Summerville and meet Anna face to face once again. To withstand the judgement of those clear blue eyes and admit out loud that in the depths of his being – or the shallows as Emily pointed out – he had been a dissembler and a liar, a half-hearted womanizer and a would-be sot, excusing himself for all his meagre excesses by pretending to be ill. There would be no possibility of the slightest subterfuge. Nothing to hide behind. Not a bit of masculine dignity remaining. He must stand before her, penitent, naked of guile as the day he was born. He owed it to the memory of Juhan.

Scribbling a hasty note for Emily: *Feeling better. Went to...* But he couldn't think of anything except the truth. And why not? *Went to see Anna Fedora*, he wrote, *to apologize.*

A FOR SALE sign was planted on her front lawn and there was no answer when he pressed the buzzer. He went around the back and cupped his hands around his eyes to peer inside. Everything looked as before. The furniture he remembered. Surely she wouldn't be gone yet. The best option seemed to be to sit and wait. Parked in front of her house, the warmth of the afternoon sun glaring through the windshield, a tad dozy – for a moment he may actually have slept – letting his mind meander to a green watercolour sea. In slow motion, just above the surface of the crusty world, he saw her running through tall beach grass. *WAIT. Wait for me*, he shouted. *ANNA*. But she was gone and he returned to the cottage, to a soft downy bed in the sleeping loft, warmed at night by solar heat and cooled during the day by the prevailing winds.

This last image turned his mind to more practical aspects, like the cost of construction and the intricacies of design. What was preventing him from actually purchasing some shore property and building a place? Others had done it. Lester Brown from the office spent every weekend working on his cabin. Charlie Moses planned to move into the house he was building out in the country when he retired. As a kid, Emmanuel had enjoyed making things from wood. Working with his hands. In Industrial Arts he hammered together quite an intricate birdhouse, a sturdy bookshelf, a mahogany sewing box lined in velvet as a Christmas present for his mother. The apex of his accomplishments in carpentry, however, was the tree house he and Donny Beener erected in the woods behind Donny's house. This was no childish affair of sticks nailed clumsily together, but a proper building with a planked floor, insulation, a real window, a hinged door and a shingled roof. Donny's dad had advised them in the construction. After it was completed, he and Donny spent many hours there consuming cans of pilfered beer, perusing old *Playboys*, practicing the aged art of rolling your own, sharing the despair and elation of puberty. His old pal, Donny Beener. Where was he now? Suddenly Emmanuel missed his boyhood friend with such stabbing pain that it brought him back once again to the reality of his grown-up circumstances, waiting in his car outside Anna Fedora's house, with the dreaded ordeal of her judgement yet before him.

It was past five when Anna finally pulled into her driveway. Emmanuel took a few deep breaths to brace himself before walking up to meet her.

"Well, well," she said, "if it isn't the Midnight Rambler. Surely they haven't removed the tumour already?"

She had turned her back to unlock the door, and he found it hard to gauge the depth of her sarcasm by the tone of her voice.

"I'm so sorry, Anna," he said. "Truly sorry. I'm actually a very honest person. Usually. I admire honesty. I came to apologize and explain, if that's possible. The whole truth and nothing but. I swear to God."

Anna led him into the living room, indicated a chair and sat down on the sofa opposite him.

"I cannot believe that Emily would involve you in our domestic dispute. You've probably gathered that things haven't been right between us for quite some time. We had a row and I did what any other red-blooded man would do – took off. It was either that or spousal violence." He chuckled to indicate that, of course, he was exaggerating, not being the type to attack a woman, his hands around his wife's smug little deceitful neck, choking the life out of her, his fist directed into her simpering face, knocking the teeth out and permanently damaging the bloodied nose. He was the type, rather, who would bang the table, causing coffee cups to tremble in their saucers. "She had no right to call you in the middle of the night."

"She was worried, Emmanuel. Surely you must understand that. And I didn't help the situation one bit by giving out false information about your test results."

"Mea culpa. My most grievous fault. All I can say as an excuse is that I had myself convinced. It's true they found nothing, but forgot to inform me of that fact and, not to my credit, I was too much of a coward to call and find out for sure. I suppose I had been looking to find something to blame for what was wrong with me: my wife, my sons, my job. A brain tumour seemed the easiest way out. Now, I'm left blaming only myself."

"What exactly do you blame yourself for, Emmanuel?" she asked.

"Everything."

She said nothing, keeping her eyes steady.

They sat in silence for some time.

"It's as if my whole past was blown to smithereens," he finally said. "Considering the sorry state of mankind in much of the world, I've been very lucky. I have nothing to complain about except my own inadequacies. Things always fell into place for me. A pattern already laid out, I just had to follow directions. I was never really conscious of making a choice. It never even occurred to me I had a choice."

"Of course you made a choice," Anna said. "Everyone does, whether conscious or not. And it must have worked for you for many years. It just may not be working for you any more. You've changed, your wife has probably changed as well. The children you raised together have gone. For every gain, there is also a loss. One side of the equation must equal the other, if you work things out correctly. Two cows are chatting across a barbed wire fence. 'Oh, to get to the other side,' says cow number one. 'You are on the other side,' says cow number two. What do you want, Emmanuel? What do you really want?"

Another long period of silence, as he tried to decide. What do I want? What do I want? Of all the questions he had to answer lately, no one had asked him that. I want what I already have. My memories. My vision of Emily as she once was, the surge of feeling I had for her, the longing for her body, the protectiveness that made me finally feel like a man. My beautiful boys – even now thinking of them bringing tears to my eyes, seeing what they have become, their earnestness, their generosity, their concern about the world. Himself and Emily, producing these precious people who never existed before. The love he felt for them went beyond anything they could say or do; it encompassed the wholeness of their being – his boys. And Emily too. She had, over the years, become a part of him. A bit headstrong, to be sure, trying so hard "to be her own person," but still, they had spent practically a lifetime together

"What I really want," he finally said, "is a dog. I've always wanted a dog. All my life I've missed having a dog. The last dog I had was old Rufus, when I was a kid."

It was a stupid answer. Lamebrain. But truly, he could think of nothing else, except to live for as long as was left to him. He already had everything he ever wanted when it came right down to it.

Anna laughed. "You truly do have an ungrasping heart, Emmanuel," she said.

All at once Emmanuel remembered the sign on the lawn. Immersed in his own turmoil, he had forgotten.

"You're selling your house? You're moving?"

"There is no longer a reason to stay."

Juhan's presence filled the room, his lively mind, his bright blue eyes, the wisdom he had gathered during his long and torturous life.

"I miss my father very much," Anna said. "In July I'm going to Estonia. To return his ashes to the place of his birth. To become Anna Lipp once again. He was already too sick to return when our homeland gained its freedom, but he always wanted to go back. I might even stay and carry on where my father left off. After fifty years of Communist occupation, there's a lot to be done. You can imagine – being a bureaucrat yourself – the incredible workload involved in setting up a new government. They can use all the help they can get, and a mathematician can also be a visionary. Everything has to be reconstructed: the postal system, taxation, real estate laws, the monetary system, public education. It's an enormous undertaking. I found out I have family there. Cousins. An aunt who is still living. When my father's obituary appeared in the Estonian newspaper, they contacted me."

"I don't want you to go," Emmanuel blurted out.

Anna laughed. "Why not come with me? I don't mind a travelling companion. If things between you and your wife are as bad as you say."

She was just testing him, he knew, to see if he had learned anything.

"Though sometimes," she went on, "quarrels are a way of working things out."

"Thanks just the same." He smiled. "But I don't know the language and am probably too old to begin learning it now."

It was the right answer. She stood up. She had forgiven him.

"I have to be honest about this," he said. "I love you, Anna Fedora. But I suppose you knew that."

"Goodbye, Emmanuel," she said, shaking his hand. "Good luck."

41

SPRING had arrived. The sun rose before seven, and didn't set again until twelve hours later, the ground was thawing, and buds appeared on the maple tree in the front yard. It was time to pack away winter. *What do you want, what do you really want, Emmanuel?* Anna's words kept repeating themselves in his mind, though he knew that his decision had been made, was, in fact, imprinted within him a long time ago, perhaps even before he was born. He was what he was, what he always had been. A family man. A man of deep commitment underneath all his whining. A loyal man. A responsible man. He could not imagine himself travelling the world in search of adventure even with Anna Fedora by his side, leaving his boys and his wife behind. It would be like cutting off his own arm. They were a part of him. I am what I am, Emmanuel thought, though not exactly the person I thought I was or wish I could be. *What you are looking for is...* Juhan had started to tell him, but he never finished and Emmanuel never asked. He had to find the answer to that question himself. Everyone did.

He called his boys. *Are you sure you're all right, Dad? Can't remember the old man ever being sick before.* "Nothing to worry about," Emmanuel reassured them. "I'm back to myself now." They were both planning to come home for a visit in the summer. Maybe they could rent a place by the sea for a week like when they were kids. Gerry would bring Pam. *I want you to meet her, Dad. I think she's the one.* "Yes," Emmanuel said, "yes, we'll do that. We'll definitely do that. I've been thinking of buying some property and building a cottage at the shore. As a weekend retreat for now. As a place to retire to in a few short years." A place for the generations yet to be born, he thought, some of whom he might be lucky enough to meet.

A vision of his family around him, grandchildren on his knee. Departing from the party hand-in-hand then, the old folks, leaving behind the young ones with their life energy still intact to continue the dance. *Goodbye. So long. Drive carefully on the way home, folks.* Maybe his own soul returning in another body. He wished he could believe that. Nature did recycle, of that he was certain, but in forms impossible for man to comprehend.

Only stubbornness kept them apart now. M and m. Play-acting. A habit of years, this period of avoidance after an argument, pretending the other didn't exist, giving things time to settle. He could see Emily's face softening, her stiff little walk returning to normal, the corner of her lip fighting off a smile. Every day had a new dawning. They would begin anew, as adults, sharing a past and a future.

There was one more thing he needed to do. Driving past Exit 13 to Banbury. Past Exit 14 to Summerville, Dexter. So long. Goodbye. Fare thee well, Anna Fedora. May all your dreams come true. You will remain in my heart forever. When I'm old and done for, with my arms strapped to the sides of a hospital bed, starving to death, perhaps it will be your name I'll be calling out: *Anna. Anna.* From the depths of memory and desire. Crying out for all those things that never were nor could be in one lifetime.

Farther down the highway, he would take a left off Exit 18 to Clearland. The sky a bright blue, the sun warm on his face. Even the scrubby trees along the roadway bearing a filigree of fresh green. Turning up the radio, opening the car window to let the warm breeze blow in. He had made it through the winter. He was alive and still intact. He had plans. He was a man on the move. They hadn't gotten to him yet and taken him away. While so many others died every day, he had been spared.

"This one's for you, Juhan," he said out loud.

The empty flat landscape. The infrequent cubes of habitation cut from the scraggy forest. Bungalows and trailers. An abandoned gas station. What did people out here do to make a living? And then he would see the driveway he remembered, leading to a small white house set back from the road. A swing set on the front lawn. A large tan dog standing on the front stoop, nosing the door and wagging his tail in anticipation of being let in.

He would drive past the house and turn around to stop on the other side of the pavement. There was no need to make himself obvious. Deal had disappeared, his request honoured. The curtain moving, a shadow in the window. Pulling up the hood release lever, getting out of the car to check the inner workings of the engine so he wouldn't appear suspicious. Someone was looking out at him now. Then the door opened to reveal a tall lanky fellow in a plaid shirt and jeans walking down the driveway.

Need some help over there? he would holler.

She would come out then too, onto the doorstep, shading her eyes. It was definitely her, but he knew she wouldn't recognize him. *John,* she would call out. *Supper is ready.*

I'll be right there, John would shout back. *Having trouble?* he would ask Emmanuel.

No. No, Emmanuel would answer, slamming down the hood. *Everything seems to be A-OK.*

He hoped so with all his heart. For her, for those two little girls, for all of them.

ACKNOWLEDGEMENTS

My heartfelt gratitude to those who read and commented upon the manuscript in its various incarnations over the years, especially to first reader Amy Lowe Baker; to the Writers' Federation of Nova Scotia for honouring my writing with two first place awards and to Jane Buss, Executive Director, for her time, compassion, expertise and support; to everyone at Breakwater Books for the kind reception.

Photo by Fran Aldercotte

SYR RUUS was born in Estonia at the start of the Second
World War. As a small child, she escaped with her mother
to Germany and then to the United States. She has lived in
Nova Scotia since 1970, working as a teacher while raising her
three children. This novel was the recipient of the H.R. (Bill)
Percy Prize from the Writers' Federation of Nova Scotia.